"I need control of this city." The sibilant words hissed in the gloom of the cavernous basement made the ranks of bowed heads shiver.

"Tell us what we must do, Master," asked a man kneeling directly before the cloaked figure.

"The pack alpha of this city and his beta must die. With them gone, the rest will follow. But are you strong enough to prevail, my furry children?"

Brown eyes, wild with fanaticism, rose to stare at the darkness within the cowl. "Their leader is old. I will force him to challenge me, and when I defeat him and gain control of the pack, I shall hand the reins of leadership over to you, Master."

"Excellent. Do not disappoint me." The unspoken words 'or else . . .' hung in the damp air. The figure in the heavy, hooded robe spun and walked to a table laden with esoteric items—skulls, crucibles, stoppered bottles—but from the panoply of objects available, he came back with a scrap of cloth. The Master dangled the fabric before the nose of his minion. "Mark this scent well, for I seek the descendent of the one who once wore this. The portents all point to her residing hereabouts. I must have her. Find the girl, but do not harm her. She is *mine*." The possessive words hung in the air, tainted with cold cruelty.

His faithful follower breathed deeply of the scent, and at his growled urging, one by one, the members of the Master's accumulated army crept forward to inhale and mark the scent.

Only once the last minion had returned to his kneeling position did the Master address them again. "Go forth, my children. Cause havoc. Take lives. Kill the leaders of the pack, but most important of all," he said, his voice low, yet resonating loudly within the minds of his followers, "find the girl."

Growls erupted and clothing flew as the ranks of kneeling men, many still boys, let their beasts—wolves with mad eyes—burst through. They raced from the underground chamber and fled to the city streets, their eerie howls rising in the night sky and announcing to all that the Master had arrived.

And he'd brought death with him.

Scared of Spiders

Eve Langlais

2nd Edition Edits by Devin Govaere
Produced in Canada

Published by Eve Langlais
1606 Main Street, PO Box 151
Stittsville, Ontario, Canada, K2S1A3
http://www.EveLanglais.com

ISBN-13: 978-1530507931
ISBN-10: 1530507936

Scared of Spiders is a work of fiction and the characters, events and dialogue found within the story are of the author's imagination and are not to be construed as real. Any resemblance to actual events or persons, either living or deceased, is completely coincidental.

Chapter One

The horrible hairy creature scurried toward her, its evil intent evident. Josie squealed and backed up, wanting to escape but too frightened to turn her back on the approaching menace. Her plump ass hit the wall. There was nowhere left to go. She closed her eyes, said a quick prayer, and stamped her foot down to end the spider's reign of terror, all the while cringing.

"Eeew! Eeew!" She hopped off the black smudge, the remains of the icky critter that dared terrorize her in her own home, and sat down hard on the couch, her whole body shaking.

For years, her father had patiently tried to explain—to deaf ears—how the spider was more scared of her. *Yeah, right.* She knew that someday one of those hairy, ugly suckers would kill her; she'd even dreamt of it. It would wrap her in a sticky cocoon, leaving only her nose and eyes uncovered. She'd have to watch as the eight-legged killer approached with its fangs bared, hungry for lunch. And, when her end came, she hoped her ghost lingered long enough for her to haunt her dad and say, "Told you so."

Josie freely admitted she wasn't a brave person, and her fear wasn't limited to spiders. Itemizing the things that freaked her out, though, would take too long, and she had an interview to get ready for. The idea of trying to sell herself and her abilities to a new employer made her nervous—make that scared the bejesus out of her—but she didn't have a choice. She'd had to quit her previous job after the owner made some unwelcome advances. She'd only barely escaped his pawing and tendered her resignation by e-mail, unwilling, and unable, to face him again.

However, her landlord wasn't likely to care that her unemployed status was because of sexual harassment. Not to mention, she still had to eat. She'd swallowed her trepidation and scoured the help-wanted ads to find the perfect job. Now, if only she could pretend confidence for her upcoming face-to-face meeting with the company owner. A meeting that she simultaneously dreaded and looked forward to, for the voice on the phone—deep and wickedly sexy—had sent shivers down her spine. The good kind. Not that she intended to date anyone she worked with. *Ha, like I'd ever muster up the courage to try.* However, it would be interesting to see if there was a hot body to match the voice. *He's probably short, has a comb-over, and is married.*

Nevertheless, she dressed carefully for the interview she'd finagled, reminding herself that this should be a piece of cake with her spotless résumé. The butterflies in her stomach mocked her inner pep talk.

Armed with a small can of Raid in her bag—perfect for muggers and bugs alike—she caught the first of two buses to reach her destination.

The company, located in a warehouse in the

docks district, wasn't exactly a prime location, but beggars without jobs couldn't be choosers. As she got off the bus, Josie eyed the gray edifice with its trademark rows of windowpanes set high and the several rollup bay doors. Since they were all shut tight, she made her way to a gray door to the side marked *Office*. After taking a deep breath, she opened the door and walked in.

Chaos met her. A noisy cacophony of forklifts, music blaring, and men talking. Really big men, who suddenly, as if controlled by one mind, stopped what they were doing and turned to look at her.

Caught by so many eyes at once, she felt like a bug under a microscope, and it took all of her will not to turn and flee. Her eyes, in a millisecond, scanned the various rugged faces turned toward her. She found herself visually captivated by one man in particular—a giant of a man whose chest strained his shirt and whose tousled dark hair begged for a hand to brush it. Within seconds of noticing this manly piece of eye candy, she found her gaze snagged by another equally big man with a carefree grin and wavy blond hair.

Logic dictated they should scare her. They were, after all, huge and eyeing her like some yummy treat that had landed in their laps, but she warmed instead under their frank appraisal. *So this is what the books mean when they talk about instant attraction.*

She'd taken a step forward, meaning to introduce herself and ask for directions to the office, when her gaze was caught by a movement in the upper corner of the vestibule. From a dusty web, layered thickly where the ceiling met the wall, dangled a spider—a huge spider—that, as if sensing her regard, spun to face her. Josie took a step back, terror riveting her in the face of the large arachnid with the hairy legs. When it began dropping down . . . *It's coming for me!* . . . all reason fled her, and she whirled to escape. Good-looking men or not, job or not, irrationality won, and she quickly exited the building to escape the eight-legged monster.

As she quick-walked her way up the sidewalk, she pondered something odd: despite her phobia, and mouth-drying fear, she had an urge to go back and somehow brave the critter waiting for her. *Damn it, I should have pulled out my Raid.* So that she could find out the names of the two men who'd woken her libido. Totally out of character, and it just went to show how attractive she'd found them. For a moment, she allowed herself a quick fantasy of dating one of those hunks, of being *his woman.* Her body shivered, pleased at the thought.

Of course, first I'd have to decide which one is hotter.

Chapter Two

He smelled her the moment she walked in—a tantalizing mix of peaches 'n' cream and woman that made his beast pace in his mind and whisper *Ours.* Clint looked up to see the face of the one he'd waited for—*my mate*—and sucked in a breath, for she wasn't what he'd expected at all.

For one, she was tiny. He doubted she'd even reach his chin, yet while short in stature, she had the curves, pillowy and sweet, of a woman. Their eyes met, and even across the space separating them, he noticed her interest, the way her lips softened and parted. An innocent look that made him rock-hard. *Oh, baby, I can't wait to see your face when it's looking up at me, glazed with passion.*

She broke the glance, and Clint realized something else before her gaze turned fearful and she whirled to escape. He wasn't the only man who'd noticed her.

But forget that dilemma for the moment. She'd left, and if he didn't hurry, he'd have to resort to sniffing out her trail like some trained canine. Clint strode across the warehouse, snarling when a few of his pack brothers moved to follow. They backed off, unwilling to challenge their alpha. Clint reached the rapidly shutting door with Brandon, best friend and pack beta, on his heels.

"She's mine," he growled at his lieutenant, who ignored his order.

"Not if I get to her first," replied Brandon, hip-checking him aside to dive through the door.

If we weren't best friends . . . Clint gritted his teeth and followed, emerging into bright sunlight. The woman he intended to bed—and, yes, wed—had already scurried half a block away. Whereas Brandon jogged to catch up to her, Clint simply stuck two fingers in his mouth and whistled.

The strident sound startled her, and she whirled to gape back at him with big, doe-like eyes.

"You wouldn't happen to be my two p.m. interview, would you?" he said on a hunch, his question loud enough for her to hear as he strolled toward her. He tried to look harmless. What a joke, she was probably right to run. *I am the big, bad wolf the stories warned you about.* She stood her ground. However, even as her fearful bearing screamed weak, but that was okay because he had strength enough for both of them.

Brandon, with his long stride and closer position, reached her first, and Clint bit back a grin as she cringed from him and clutched her purse tightly to her chest.

"I'm Brandon Schuster," said his business partner, sticking his hand out. She hesitated, biting her lower lip before placing her trembling hand in Brandon's.

The shock of their skin-to-skin contact was all too visible, and Clint held back an urge to rip her away from his beta. His beast snarled in his mind, willing to forgo friendship so it might take a bite out of the one who dared touch their woman. Ignoring the bloodthirsty requests of his beast, Clint instead smiled widely at the petite woman, perhaps a tad toothily, judging by the wide eyes that rose to meet his.

"Hi, there. I'm Clint Jefferson, majority owner of J&S Inc." He added that last bit on purpose and enjoyed the way Brandon's mouth tightened. Clint stuck his hand out, and with the same lip-biting trepidation, she placed her hand in his. An electric current shot through him, and his beast grunted in recognition. *Ours.* Expected, and yet odd, because there was no doubting the same thing had happened with Brandon, who now frowned at him.

His tiny woman snatched her hand back and took a step away from them, her gaze darting between them, but he was glad to notice her initial trepidation seemed to have faded. And if he wasn't mistaken, he could smell distinct interest, from her lower parts anyway.

"I'm Josephine Winters, and I'm sorry to have wasted your time." Her voice, no surprise, was soft and demure, kind of like her.

It's always the quiet ones, though, that end up wildest in bed. Clint forced himself to focus on her words instead of how she'd look naked and bent over. *Delicious.* "Why do you say that? Your résumé is quite impressive. Not only are you familiar with the computer system we're on, you've spent several years in management. It's exactly what we're looking for."

"But—" Again she gnawed, which exposed her pearly whites, and Clint really had to restrain himself from joining her in chewing on her full lower lip.

Brandon jumped in to help. "I admit we look like a noisy bunch, but I promise you, our staff will obey you."

Clint silently agreed, for if they didn't, they'd face the wrath of their pack alpha.

Her spine straightened, and her countenance went from soft to indignant.

Hmm, looks like my intended mate might have a backbone hidden in there. It made him wonder what other surprises her meek exterior hid.

"It's not that," she said. "I know I can do the job."

"Then what's the problem?" he asked. Whatever the problem, he'd fix it. He couldn't let Josephine—such a big name for a tiny thing—walk away.

"You'll laugh," she said, staring down at the ground, her shoulders slumping as she shuffled her feet.

Clint wanted to sweep her up and carry her away. There was something about her timid nature that made his protective side swell. "I promise I won't," he said and was echoed by Brandon.

"You have spiders," she whispered, unable to look them in the eyes.

"Spiders?" repeated Brandon, incomprehension on his face. "Well, yeah. They come in with the shipments."

Clint saw her flinch and held on to his urge to laugh. Although spiders didn't bother him, it looked as though Josephine was terrified of them, and there was no denying their place had a fair share. Despite the connection he felt drawing him to her, Clint had to wonder at the choice of her as his mate. *If she's scared of spiders, then how the hell is she ever going to accept the fact that I turn furry on the full moon?*

Again, a dilemma for later, for now that he'd found his female—*my mate*—he wanted her where he could keep an eye on her, not to mention having her around would make it easier to seduce her. *And protect what is mine.*

"If spiders are the problem, then I think we can do something about that. Come back with us, and we'll discuss it in our office. Brandon will go ahead and clear the way. And I promise tonight, even if it takes a whole case of bug spray, we will blanket the place from top to bottom and get rid of the critters."

Her eyes widened in surprise, and her lips curved into a sweet smile that made his cock jerk. *Damn, she's a hottie. I am going to have to find more reasons to make her smile.*

"You'd do that for me?" she said incredulously. "But you don't even know me. And surely you've got other applicants for the job."

"We need you," Clint said, the words sincere, even if he meant them for something else.

"Do we ever," muttered Brandon. Clint shot him a hard glare, which Brandon pretended to ignore.

How is it possible we both feel drawn to the same woman? If she were a bitch in heat, I'd understand it, but I've never heard of a human attracting more than one werewolf mate. One alpha was hard enough to handle; throw in a beta who could have been alpha, and any woman, werewolf bitch or not, would have her hands full. *In that case, I'll just have to make sure that she chooses me over Brandon.*

As they neared the entrance to the warehouse, Brandon jogged ahead. Soon exaggerated stomping sounds drifted through the open door along with shouted orders to clear out any webs, along with their inhabitants.

"You guys are nuts," she muttered, but Clint caught the slight smile hovering around her lips.

"All clear," shouted Brandon.

When Josephine hesitated at the doorway, Clint grabbed her hand and tugged her in after him. She followed him meekly, her cheeks pink and her eyes downcast, which was probably a good thing because every pack member in the place noticed her. Their eyes tracked her, and Clint could see their interest and, in a few cases, their beasts as they struggled with their human half.

Josephine might appear fragile, but something about her appealed to the rough crew ,who by nature of blood, were like family to him. However blood didn't quell jealousy. *She is mine, and my brothers better have the sense to keep away.* His beast stirred in his mind and growled in agreement.

Clint didn't let go of her hand until he had closed the door to the upstairs office behind them. He'd no sooner ushered her into a chair than Brandon breezed in with a grin and perched himself on the edge of Clint's desk.

Josephine huddled in the chair, her lip-biting trepidation back, but he also smelled the desire and was jolted to realize some of her shyness might stem from her reaction to them. She probably had a strong desire to touch them, an urge she couldn't understand. An overwhelming desire for contact that Clint—and, he'd bet, Brandon—fought. Even though he'd known vaguely what to expect when he met *the one*, there was no denying words couldn't adequately describe it.

"So, when can you start?" Clint asked when the silence drew out.

Her brows creased in a frown. "Don't you want to ask me some questions first?"

"Are you single?" blurted Brandon, which made Josephine's eyes widen.

Clint bit back a curse, even as he wanted the answer. He hurried to cover his friend's gaffe. "What he means to say is sometimes we need to work late and that a significant other might object."

His explanation eased some of the tension in her shoulders. "Oh. I don't have anyone waiting for me at home except for my cat, so working late isn't an issue."

A cat? Clint's beast snorted in disdain, and Clint fought not to smile. His wolf had little use or like for felines. *I wonder how she feels about canines with great big teeth.* Clint proceeded to ask her proper interview questions, ignoring Brandon's puzzled glances. His best friend didn't have a subtle bone in his body.

She relaxed, and when it came to talking about her skills, he found the confidence he'd thought she lacked. That confidence shriveled when he said, "So, I guess I should ask why you left your last position."

He caught the quick flash of fear and disgust in her eyes, and he bit back a growl. *Mental note to self—look up her previous place of employment and kick the ass of the jerk who forced her to quit.*

She took a deep breath. "The owner decided that when his secretary quit I should assume her . . . " She blushed, and Clint clenched his fists under the desk as he suddenly had a vivid image of what had happened. "Um, let's just say I had no interest in the extra duties he thought I should provide."

"Well, you don't have to worry about that kind of thing happening here. We have no formal rule on dating coworkers, but if anyone harasses you, just let me know, and he'll be dealt with." *On the end of my fist.*

"Thank you." She met his gaze, and it was like a punch to the gut.

I must have her.

Brandon clasped his hands together and rubbed them. "Well, since that's all settled, how about I give Josephine here a tour and introduce her to the boys?"

"I don't actually use *Josephine*. It's too long and stuffy. I usually go by Josie."

"Then Josie it is," said Brandon as he tugged her up from the chair and tucked her arm into the crook of his. With a wink at Clint, he left with her. Meanwhile, Clint clenched his fists in an effort to not run after them and tear his beta from her. His beast didn't like her leaving their sight—unmarked and in the company of another—and paced restlessly inside him.

Let him have his moment because I'll get mine later when I give Josie a ride home. And, hopefully soon, the leather seat in my SUV won't be the only thing she's sitting on. His cock hardened in anticipation.

Chapter Three

Josie tried to concentrate on what Brandon showed her and the men he introduced her to, but the only thing she registered was how his simple presence and glancing touches made her blood boil. *What is wrong with me? Here I've lucked out and landed a job, yet all I can think of is how those lips of his would taste.* The urge to touch him overwhelmed her, and she fought it by stuffing her hands into her jacket pockets. It didn't help that he touched her often, brief brushes of his hand and body that made her jump and, to her embarrassment, wet her panties. *God, I hope he doesn't realize just how much he flusters me.*

Eventually the tour ended, and she found herself back in Clint's equally disturbing presence. Darker of countenance with brooding eyes, he didn't even have to touch her for the shivers to dance down her spine and spiral into her cleft.

"Brandon, I'm going to run Josie home. Could you make sure her office is ready for the morning?"

Trapped in the close confines of a car with my new, super-sexy boss? I can't. I'll melt into a puddle for sure. "Oh, no. You don't have to drive me anywhere. I'm perfectly fine taking transit."

"It's not a problem. Besides, we can talk more

about the job on the way. Shall we?" He held open the office door for her, and she thought she caught him smirking at Brandon, who didn't look happy all of a sudden. But she had little time to ponder their strange interplay, for she found herself ushered down the stairs and out a rear door to a gated parking lot.

He led her to a large black vehicle. He opened the passenger door for her, and she climbed into the luxury vehicle in a state of bemusement. When he seated himself on the driver's side, the large SUV grew small at his overwhelming masculine presence. Josie clutched her hands together nervously, her palms damp. What a strange day. Her new employers seemed remarkable, and not just because they'd taken her fear of spiders in stride. Each had to be the most handsome man she'd ever met, and nice, too.

And much as she fought her attraction to them, if she weren't mistaken, the interest was reciprocated, judging by their facial and body language. It should have frightened her. *I don't date big, larger-than-life men.* But given her body's reaction to them, maybe she should. Even with the knowledge that they were her employers, their interest in her as a woman didn't inspire repugnance, nor did it make her bristle at what some women would perceive as inappropriate sexual interest. On the contrary, she would find it hard to refuse should either of them ask her on a date. However, difficult as it would be to say no, she would, for they were her bosses and she knew better than to mix business with pleasure. *I need this job, and having sex with either of them would jeopardize that. A pity, though, because never before have I understood what it meant to be in lust.*

She needed to stop thinking of them as possible lovers. She was their employee, even if their job offer, so enthusiastically given, stunned her. Not only was her salary much more than she'd expected, they'd given her an office of her own, along with free rein to peruse their operations and streamline them. *Such confidence in me. I don't get it, but at the same time, I love it.*

Despite her admonishments to her libido to think of them as her bosses, seated so close to Clint, she couldn't stop the wet warmth that seeped into her panties. Nor could she think of a thing to say other than, "You need to turn left at the next set of lights."

Scintillating conversation to be sure. He pulled up at her direction in front of the white vinyl triplex where she lived on the third floor.

"Thank you," she said as she ducked her chin down to avoid his mesmerizing green eyes. She pulled on the door handle, and as soon as it had swung open, he appeared, hand extended to help her out.

Goodness, he moves fast. Placing her hand in his, she again experienced the same electrical jolt of earlier, a jolt that zinged through her body and sizzled in her cleft. *Oh my.* She blushed when she felt the rush of moisture, glad in the encroaching twilight that he couldn't see how his simple touch affected her. *His and Brandon's.* For, strangely enough, she experienced the same erotic effect when he touched her.

"What time would you like me to pick you up in the morning?" Clint asked as she fumbled her key out to unlock the door.

"Excuse me?" She regarded him blankly. "Why would you pick me up?"

"You don't have a car, so I'll just swing by on my way in to work and grab you."

Josie frowned. "You don't have to do that. I'm perfectly fine taking public transit." *Not to mention, with the way I keep wetting my panties around you, I'll need to bring a change for when I get to the office. Make that several pairs.*

"I insist. Besides, you're on my way. I'll see you tomorrow morning at eight." With a wave and a smile that made her panties wet enough to wring, he climbed back into his SUV and zoomed away, leaving Josie flabbergasted on her stoop.

"Nuts. They're both nuts," she muttered as she wandered into her apartment. A streak of gray fur came bolting toward her, and Josie bent to catch her furry dynamo.

"Hello, Snickers," she murmured against the soft fur. "Great news. I've got a job working for the two handsomest guys ever."

As she talked aloud to her cat and bustled about making them dinner, she couldn't help thinking of Clint and Brandon, their charismatic presence imprinted on her. *And what's up with the electrical shocks when they touch me?*

It was like something out of a romance novel, but as Josie reminded herself, this was real life, and while men like her new bosses might find her timid exterior a challenge, it wouldn't be long after they caught her that they would let her go for greener pastures. *I am not the kind of girl who can keep the attention of men like that.* At least, she never had in the past. *I wonder if it would be different with them since, this time, I'm the one who's lusting.* Foolish thinking that she had to forget. *I could never hope to keep a guy like that for long.*

But, damn, the heartbreak would probably be worth the wildest naked ride of her life.

Chapter Four

Clint headed back to his house, a ranch outside the city limits with acres of land and plenty of space to accommodate others of his kind when they came to visit. He wasn't surprised to find Brandon waiting for him on the front porch. Clint grinned at him, for, despite their new rivalry for the chance to win Josie, they were best friends and competition was the norm.

"Smooth move getting her to ride home with you," said Brandon grudgingly as he followed him inside.

Clint grabbed them both a beer before dropping his bomb with a smile. "And I'll be picking her up in the morning."

"W-what?" Brandon sputtered. "I checked out her file when you left and saw where she lives. How the fuck did you convince her to ride with you, considering you live on the opposite side of town?"

Clint shrugged. "I didn't tell her that part. So don't ruin it. I don't like the idea of her being on public transit with no one to watch over her."

Brandon scowled. "Fine, but you're going to share the driving duties with me."

Clint didn't like it, but when he won Josie, he didn't want Brandon calling foul. "Deal. Talking about sharing, what are we going to do about Josie? We both obviously want her, which, I've got to admit, surprises me considering she's human." *A really yummy-smelling one.*

"Yeah, that kind of surprised me, too. I always expected to get paired up with some Amazon blonde. Not that I'm complaining. Josie's got curves begging to be driven."

Clint growled, unable to stop the sound at hearing Brandon talk so blatantly about his mate. "Sorry. I hear you talk about her, and my wolf goes nuts."

"I know the feeling," said Brandon, who then took a swig of his beer.

"What do you mean? Are you feeling the urge too?" It didn't really surprise him. It happened often in packs that alpha's and betas who were deeply bonded often felt the need to claim the same woman. The real question was, who would actually win her as his mate?

"Much as I hate to suggest it, given the way we both feel, we could share her or take turns. But given her timid nature, I don't get the impression she'd be into that." Having partaken in threesomes before, Clint wasn't averse to it, especially with Brandon acting as the second man. *I'm not into guys touching me, but watching a woman pleasuring another guy or seeing her being pleasured up close and personal is totally fucking hot.*

Brandon shrugged. "So, we let her decide which one of us she wants." He smiled wickedly. "And may the best wolf win."

Clint groaned. "Dammit, that brings up

another problem. She's not a shifter. How the hell are we going to break the news to her about our furry side without her freaking out? You saw how she reacted to spiders. Can you imagine what she'll do when she finds out we're werewolves?"

"So, we don't show her our wolves until after we've gotten her to trust us and bedded her."

Clint somehow doubted it would end up that simple. *Although under that veneer of fear, I get the impression there might be a core of steel. She might just need a little encouragement to bring it out. And the best place to start is in bed.*

Chapter Five

Josie's first week at work flew by. True to his word, Clint picked her up every morning, with coffee, which by some miracle he'd figured out she took with two creams, one sugar. In the evenings, Brandon, with a grin and crooked elbow, escorted her home in his sports car, which, after the first terrifying ride, she admitted was actually exhilarating, especially when he took the corners fast and tight.

At work, they were professional—most of the time. She gained confidence as her suggestions for improvement were listened to and implemented. She smiled at the lingering scent of Raid every time she entered her office. And while she'd found herself uncomfortable the first day under the scrutiny of the men on staff, by the second day they nodded at her respectfully and called her *ma'am*, which she found entertaining, considering they all towered over her by a good foot or more.

She reorganized the workplace to her liking, her usual shyness disappearing as she found her groove. *I am good at what I do.* She even had a nickname by the end of her first week, which made her grin when she escaped to her office to work—Little General. *I might be short and scared of spiders and stuff, but when it comes to organization, I rock.*

The only stressful moment came about a week after she started. Hugging her clipboard while barking orders that made the men scurry, she heard a voice that sent slimy fingers tickling up her spine.

"Josephine, so glad I found you," said a familiar nasal voice.

Josie whirled to see the balding, pudgy form of her previous boss. "What are you doing here?"

"You wouldn't take my calls. Lucky me, one of the drivers told me you were working here." Her sweating ex-boss beamed at her, and Josie took a step back, her shoulders hunching.

"What do you want? I have work to do." She tried to sound brusque, but instead, her voice came out reedy and thin. She still remembered the way he'd cornered her and, with a salacious look, propositioned her, his rough hands pinching her as she pushed past him to escape.

"I want you to come back. I'm even prepared to increase your salary," he announced magnanimously.

Josie shook her head. "No thank you. I like it here."

The jovial look on her ex-employer's face darkened, and his piggy eyes narrowed. "Listen here, missy. Either you take my offer, or I'll—"

She never got a chance to find out what the 'or else' part was because Clint, his face reflecting the thunderous expression in his eyes—and looking totally hot—picked her ex-boss up by the material of his jacket and shook him.

"Just what do you think you're doing coming in here and threatening my wo—employee?"

Josie knew she should protest, but honestly, she quite enjoyed watching the perverted bully getting his comeuppance.

"I-I…"

Fabric tore, and her ex-employer, not looking so threatening anymore, dropped to the ground. He scrambled to his feet, only to have Brandon grab him by the nape of the neck and propel him out of the nearest open bay.

Brandon came back, a grin on his face, while Clint gazed down at her with concern. "Are you okay? Do you want me to go out and smack him around for you?"

Josie was stunned speechless at the way they'd both come to her rescue, but inside, her heart swelled. And in that moment, she realized something shocking. She was falling in love—with both of them.

Flustered, she muttered her thanks with red cheeks and downcast eyes. She fled to her office as soon as she could, feeling the burning weight of their stares at her back.

I must be going nuts. Falling in love with two men who, while kind and courteous themselves, have yet to ask me out on a date. Crazy or not, her burgeoning feelings made her more determined than ever to work hard and prove herself to them. And that was why she ended up going in on a Saturday when the company was closed to get some extra work done.

She was deep into her spreadsheets when the murmur of voices caught her attention. She ignored them, even as her body flushed in interest, wondering if it was one of her good-looking bosses.

Ignorance removed itself from the list of options when the first savage snarl sounded from the warehouse floor.

Oh my God, what was that?

Chapter Six

Clint and Brandon filed into the warehouse, followed by the rest of the pack. A shiver ran through Brandon as the lingering scent of Josie hit his nostrils. He breathed deeply. Damn, it was as if she'd just walked by, and the sweet aroma, uniquely hers, made him hard, even given the reason for their presence at the warehouse on a weekend.

"Do you really think they're going to show up?" Brandon asked Clint as he leaned against some stacked crates. He hoped the rogues showed up quickly so they could take care of business and still salvage enough of the evening for him to "drop by" Josie's place with a movie and a pizza. The whole going slow so as to not scare her was chafing to both him and his beast, which whined to mark her. He could sense the impatience in Clint, too, the only saving grace in their battle to win her affections.

"Oh, they'll show," said Clint, his expression hard. "I made the message pretty clear. Meet us on our terms, or we'd take their no-show as an act of war."

"Should have gone for war," grumbled Brandon. "You know these rejects aren't going to join the pack. And even if they leave town, they'll just end up terrorizing another place." The rogues had caught their attention when they'd shown up in their town a week or so back and didn't follow pack protocol by checking in with the alpha for the area. They'd further broken pack rules by hunting without permission and causing bodily harm to a human. Unacceptable, hence the summons for them to appear and face judgment.

"My pack. My rules. Besides, I get the feeling there's another player guiding them. Rogues aren't usually so brazen."

"Speaking of which . . ." Brandon trailed off and stood up straight as he took his position of beta beside his alpha. The rogues came slinking in, a juvenile-looking bunch with greasy hair and biker-styled clothing. Wannabes who, in their very arrogance, were dangerous. Brandon still thought killing them all was the best option. If someone was pulling their strings, that would send the message of "fuck off or die," too.

But then again, his kill-now, oops-later attitude was why he wasn't pack leader. He'd let Clint enjoy the headaches. Besides, while Clint was occupied with pack politics, it left Brandon more time to pursue their little mouse, whose commanding tone in the office was at odds with her timid nature outside the workplace. But the occasional spark of attitude proved she was coming around. Slowly.

The rogue leader sauntered up to them with a cocky grin on his face. "So, who's the old guy in charge?"

Clint gave the arrogant pup a cold smile. "Me. Why? You think you can take me?"

The smile on the young rogue's face didn't

falter, and Brandon wanted to shake his head at the stupidity. Youth was well and good, but Clint was just entering his prime, and aside from his experience, he outweighed the pup by several stones.

"Name the place, old man, and I'll whip your ass for control of the pack." The challenger and his lackeys laughed amidst the growls of the pack. The pup laughed louder at the encouragement of his mangy followers, and it was then that Brandon noticed something disturbing. While all their faces were twisted in a rictus of laughter, their eyes shone with madness and, in some cases, even tinges of fear.

Brandon wished he knew sign language so he could have flashed some secret signs to Clint and warned him to watch for treachery. It was becoming more and more obvious the rogues were merely puppets, and the power to control that many meant a strong player had entered the fray without announcing themselves. *Bad manners.*

"Choose your body," said Clint, his tone hard and his posture brooking no nonsense.

"Wolf of course." The young rogue grinned as he stripped out of his clothes to reveal a lean, muscled body that, without its concealing layers, appeared even smaller.

Clint, on the other hand, once stripped, looked even more imposing with bulging muscles all over, which Brandon grudgingly admired. *No matter how much I work out, I don't have the build for that kind of bulk.*

Clint's shift into his wolf—a huge black monster with intense glowing green eyes—was effortless. The pup, on the other hand, really had to force his beast to emerge, a painful process that just reinforced Brandon's impression that the rogue group didn't act of their own wills.

Clint sat on his hairy haunches and waited for the smaller wolf to attack, which it did with the rabid intensity of a pit bull. However, it was clear from the onset what the outcome of the fight would be.

Clint's wolf let the young one snarl and snap then, in a show of force meant to intimidate, flattened the pup in one fell swoop. With his massive jaw, he pinned the other wolf by the throat to the floor.

That should have ended it. Instead, it acted like an invisible switch, and Brandon barely had time to shift, his clothes tearing as his wolf shoved through. Just in time, too, for the pack of rogues, shifting in a burst of fabric, attacked.

Brandon actually enjoyed putting the mangy pack in their place. And he would have emerged unscathed if a gasp of fright hadn't distracted him. He turned his head to see Josie, with her eyes wide and a hand clapped over her mouth, watching them from the stairs to the office.

A second later, his inattention caused a wolf flying at him to knock him down, sharp teeth snapping at his throat. Brandon scrabbled for the upper paw and regained it in time to hear Josie shriek.

A quick glance showed his little mouse standing with terrified eyes halfway down the steps to the office, a snarling wolf advancing toward her.

Done playing, Brandon snapped the neck of the wolf under him and bolted for the stairs. Clint was a black streak beside him. Brandon got there first and grabbed the foreleg of the rogue menacing Josie.

He yanked down the mutt who thought to go after his woman. As he subdued the young pup, he saw Clint shift back into human shape in time to grab Josie as she slumped in a faint.

Hmm, guess we'll have some explaining to do when she wakes up.

Chapter Seven

A glance at the stairs showed Josie, frozen with fright and with good reason, considering the wolf advancing on her. Clint ran for her, and when Brandon took care of the rogue, Clint shifted back to his man shape in time to catch Josie, whose eyes rolled up into her head as she fainted.

"Fuck." He scooped her up and gave a quick glance to the battle winding up below—less a battle and more of a massacre. *What were the pups thinking?* Brandon, still in wolf shape, met his gaze and yipped. Satisfied that Brandon would take care of the rogues still kicking, Clint carried his sleeping beauty up to his office. He laid her tenderly on the couch and hurried to pull his spare clothes out. But he wasn't quick enough.

He heard her gasp and turned while still pulling up his pants. Her startled glance settled on his still mostly naked body, and her mouth formed an *O*. She stared at his bared upper body then trailed down to stop at the bared triangle visible at the front of his pants. Clint buttoned with difficulty, given his engorging state. Her cheeks reddened, and her flustered gaze shifted to look at everything but him.

"It's okay to look," he teased as he tried to lighten the mood before the inevitable questions began. "Heck, you can even touch."

The color on her face deepened, but despite her embarrassment, the sweet scent of her desire wafted up, and Clint grinned wolfishly. *Okay, so she still wants me. Now to explain the fact we're all werewolves.*

"Um, I'm sorry to have intruded on your dog fight," she said as she fidgeted on the couch, still not meeting his gaze.

"Come on; don't play dumb. I know you saw us and the truth of what we are."

"I don't know what you're talking about," she said, lying badly.

"Josie," he cajoled. She refused to meet his eyes. He knelt in front of her and forced her to meet his gaze. "Josie, baby, you're not crazy."

"I wouldn't be so sure," she retorted. "Because I thought I saw a wolf turn into a man, and that's just nuts."

"Not nuts. You didn't mistake what you saw. We're werewolves," he said with a shrug and then held his breath as he waited for her reaction.

She opened and shut her mouth several times at his claim, clearly searching for words. Before she could say anything, Brandon walked into the office, his low-slung jeans and bare chest momentarily capturing Josie's attention before her trademark blush and shyness made her turn away.

"So, how's the news of our furriness coming along?" asked Brandon, looking between them with curiosity.

Josie didn't answer, so Clint did. "I think our Little General here is having a hard time with the concept."

Fire sparked in her eyes and her tone when she spoke. "I get the concept fine. You're both werewolves. What I want to know is how, why, and what's going to happen to me?"

"The how is I was born this way while Brandon here was bitten."

"You mean if that wolf had bitten me, I'd be a werewolf, too?" she squeaked.

"Maybe. But not likely. It takes, at the very least, an alpha to change a person, and even then, it's fifty/fifty whether the human they bite will turn." *And those who didn't died.*

"So, your saliva is dangerous?" she queried, her telltale blush pinking again.

Clint hastened to clarify. "Only when we're in wolf shape can our saliva, introduced into the blood stream of a human, change a person." He neglected mentioning the fatal aspect. It shook Clint to realize that the rogue wolf, with one bite, could have taken her from them. It also made him question whether or not he'd ever have the guts to attempt to change her. She was so frail; what if they tried and she died? He couldn't take the chance, but then again, if he didn't, she'd never bear his pups and would live the short lifespan of a human. A catch-22 either way.

"Oh, good to know. So I guess, now that you've told me your secrets, you're going to kill me." She hunched in on herself, and Clint couldn't help himself.

He laughed. "Oh, baby, you are so cute. No, we're not going to kill you."

"Definitely not," added Brandon. "Although I'm not averse to biting."

Josie's head snapped back up in shock that turned into a grudging smile as she saw Brandon's grin.

Clint chuckled. "Ignore him. He's just kidding."

"No, I'm not. I love to nibble on that soft spot on the back of a woman's neck. . . . " Suddenly realizing he might be saying too much, Brandon shut up.

Clint sat down beside her on the couch and, hoping she wouldn't flinch or bolt, slid an arm around her frail shoulders. To his surprise, after an initial stiffness, she leaned into him and laid her head on his shoulder.

"I've got to admit," said Clint, awed that she still seemed to trust him after they'd revealed their secret, "you're taking this awfully well. Most women would have run screaming."

"Promise not to laugh?" she said, her voice uncertain. "But even knowing the two of you can change into wolves with big teeth, you don't scare me."

Clint's heart almost stopped at her admission.

"Truly?" Brandon knelt at her feet and looked at her with longing in his eyes. A sentiment Clint echoed. *She accepts us. How unexpected and remarkable.*

Josie nodded her head. "Weird, huh, especially considering I'm the girl who runs from spiders."

No, not so weird because you belong to us. But I think I'll keep that revelation for another day.

"Well, that's the great thing about knowing werewolves; we make great spider killers," Brandon said with a grin.

And mates, thought Clint. "Brandon, I'm going to run Josie home. Can you make sure the mess downstairs is taken care of?" He could see his beta bristle at the order to stay behind, but one of them needed to ensure the rogues were taken care of. That was, killed. He didn't want to risk a single one of them bringing word of Josie's existence back to whomever controlled them.

Brandon understood the need and gave him a quick nod.

To spare Josie any visual trauma—the blood splatter and sprawled bodies still decorating the warehouse below—he took her out via the rear fire exit. To his surprise, she said not a word about their strange route to his SUV. Actually, she was very quiet.

Once he got the SUV on the road, he broke the silence. "Tell me what you're thinking."

"Oh, just wishful thinking."

"About?" *Me and you naked* was the answer he hoped for.

"I wondered what if would be like to be a werewolf and not be scared of stuff."

"Being a shifter doesn't make fear go away."

"But it would help, I imagine," she replied dryly.

She had a point. "Courage doesn't come from a layer of fur and teeth; courage comes from inside."

"Yeah, well, apparently the creator forgot to give me my dose."

Clint chuckled. "Baby, I think you're plenty brave. I mean look at the way you run the place, ordering those big bad wolves around like trained puppies."

She blushed. "That's different. It's work and has nothing to do with bravery."

"Really?" he said, turning to look at her. "Tell that to my last two managers. I'd just about given up hope on getting someone with the right skills when you came along. And, guess what, you might be human, but you get the job done."

"Great. But I still wish I had the other type of courage so I don't turn into a blubbering mess when a spider pops out of nowhere," she said with a grimace.

"If you don't mind me asking, where did your fear of arachnids come from?"

"Would you believe from a nightmare?" She squirmed in her seat. "It's dumb, I know, but I've had this recurring dream since my mom died when I was a little girl. As you might have guessed, it has a spider in it, and, well, let's just say it's gruesome. Ever since the nightmares started, I freak out at the sight of bugs, spiders being the worst."

"As long I'm around, I promise to protect you from eight-legged freaks." He managed to say it without laughing, but his lips twitched when she scowled at him.

"That is so not funny."

Clint chuckled. "Sorry. I loved that movie."

She tried to keep the scowl, but his humor ended up contagious, and she giggled. "Thanks for not making too much fun of me. Just for that, the next time you get fleas, I'll help you put your collar on." She'd no sooner said the words than she clapped a hand over her mouth and her eyes widened.

Clint howled. "Oh, baby, I am really starting to think you're not timid at all. It's an act to hide your wicked side."

She took her hand away from her face and smiled. "Only with you and Brandon. You both make me feel . . ." Her brow scrunched up as she tried to find a word.

"Like you've come home," he murmured.

She turned startled eyes to him, but he avoided the question he could sense on the tip of her tongue. *I don't think she's quite ready for the whole "fate has decreed you my mate" thing yet.* But he couldn't resist dropping a light kiss on her lips. The brief contact sizzled, and he wanted more, but not in the car like a teenager. He made it out of and around the car in time to help her out, and then he walked her to her door. He grabbed her keys from her trembling hands, enjoying the fact that his touch had unbalanced her as well.

In a deft movement, he unlocked her door and opened it. Before she could escape to the safety and normality of her home though, he spun her and crushed her to him.

I'm done fantasizing and fist pumping. The thing I feared most, her rejecting me because of my inner beast, is no longer an issue. And, besides, I can't wait to taste her anymore.

Chapter Eight

He's going to kiss me. And not a brief peck like he'd given her in the SUV, which, though short, had sizzled. Josie's heart rate sped up, and she tilted her head to look up at him. His green eyes blazed, and he looked as if he would speak, but as if thinking better of it, he, instead, dipped his head to kiss her.

Forget the foolish fumbles of her teenage years and the inept gropings of her adult ones. In Clint's arms, Josie discovered what the kiss of a man should feel like. Fire: unadulterated, skin-scorching, tummy-twisting, panty-wetting fire. He kissed her as if she were the most desirable woman in existence. He devoured her lips as if they were the most decadent treat imaginable. And when he pressed her against the hardness of his desire—*for me*—she mewled in want. Crazy, inexplicable, this insane attraction between them made no sense, but, oh, did she want more.

She clung to him, pressed herself against his solid body, hating all the clothes that stood between them.

A spitting hiss sounded, along with a yelp. Clint drew back from her to glare at his feet. Befuddled, Josie followed the direction of his look and saw her cat Snickers with her fur standing on end, growling and hissing at Clint.

"Snickers," she admonished, extricating herself from his embrace to pick up her extremely unhappy cat. Snickers, however, wasn't interested in cuddles. With a swipe of her paw at Josie's hands, she bolted with a trailing *yeowl* into the apartment. "Sorry about that. I guess she doesn't like wolves," said Josie with a shrug, not able to completely stifle the smile that tilted her lips.

Clint's lips quirked, and she shivered at the burning look in his eyes. "Don't worry. By the morning, I'm sure we'll have come to an agreement."

Josie blushed at his unspoken words. *Let him stay the night?* She was tempted. Throw caution to the wind and indulge in what would surely be the most erotic experience of her life, but when reality finally intruded, where would she stand? Probably on the outskirts watching and, if she was still employed, crying as Clint ended up eventually turning to another woman. Another werewolf with courage like him. "I . . . I'm sorry. I like you, really I do, but so much has happened and so fast and . . ."

He swooped down and shut her up with a hard kiss. "No, I'm sorry. I didn't mean to rush you. Go have a hot bath, relax, and I'll see you tomorrow."

It wasn't until she shut the door—after another befuddling kiss that turned her legs to wobbly noodles—that she processed his words.

But tomorrow is Sunday. Was he coming back? Would he kiss her again? *I really shouldn't let him because, honestly, I know there's no way I can keep a man like him forever. I'm just not interesting or brave enough. How tempting, though, to indulge in the pleasure he offers, even knowing of the heartbreak and disappointment that will eventually follow.*

Speaking of disappointment, what about Brandon? I guess by kissing Clint, and really, really liking it, I've made my choice. She couldn't deny the way Clint made her body sing. She also wasn't a slut to toy with two men at once, even as she found herself attracted to them both. Honor and decency stated she not lead Brandon on, even if she hadn't decided whether or not to take things further with Clint. She hoped only that Brandon wouldn't take offense.

If I were a braver woman, more of a femme fatale, I wouldn't bother deciding between two. I'd take them both to bed.

On that naughty, erotically pleasing thought, she went to sleep and had very pleasant dreams indeed for a change.

Chapter Nine

Brandon stood with his arms crossed over chest in front of the rogue when Clint returned to the warehouse. "I see you left one alive," Clint stated with flinty eyes.

"Not for long," growled Brandon with clear menace. He'd found the unconscious rogue during cleanup and held off killing him in the hopes they could get some answers.

The rogue wolf stared at the ceiling with a half-smile and didn't utter a sound. Brandon didn't like it. A normal person—especially a shifter—would attempt to struggle, plead, or even try to strike a deal. The eerie stillness the pup displayed while Brandon manhandled and trussed his ass to a chair was unnatural.

"Has he said anything?" Clint asked.

"Actually, I was just about to start the questioning. I wanted to make sure the pack had the cleanup under control." That and Brandon didn't trust himself not to kill the rogue for daring to have threatened Josie. When it came to his little mouse, his protective side knew no bounds. With Clint here, he'd have someone to rein him in if the greasy pup said the wrong thing.

Clint gripped the pup's chin and forced him

to face him. "What's your name?"

The rogue's eyes came into focus, and the smile on his face deepened. "Lucky me, if it isn't the alpha himself. The name is Joe."

"Who do you answer to?"

Joe rolled his eyes and smirked. "Wrong question."

A frown creased Clint's face, a scowl that had made more than one shifter roll over and bare his belly, but Joe just laughed. The alpha wasn't the only one who didn't appreciate it. Brandon didn't like the sound and showed his displeasure by swinging a fist and cracking it against Joe's jaw.

"Answer him," he growled.

But Joe, flexing his jaw, just laughed louder, a strident sound that irritated the ears like nails on a chalkboard.

Abruptly the mirth cut off, and the rogue's face turned serious. More disturbing, though, was the way his eyes bled from brown to pure black. Joe spoke, but Brandon shivered at the words, for it became evident that Joe was no longer home.

"Stupid dogs. It's not who I am that matters but what I want. Have you figured it out yet?"

Clint bent down until his face was inches from Joe's. "Since we're so dumb, why don't you explain it to us?"

Laughter erupted again, a chilling sound that Brandon gritted his teeth against. "He's fucking with us. Let's just kill him."

"Please do," begged Joe. "I shan't miss this one or his incompetent brothers. And besides, there's plenty more dogs for the taking. Perhaps you'd like to offer yourselves up in their place."

Clint growled. "Never. And I promise, whatever and whoever you are, I will kill you."

"But first you have to find me." Chilling laughter erupted, and Brandon wanted to clap his hands over his ears at the madness in the sound. Joe's body trembled in its bonds, and his eyes rolled up in his head. Harder and harder he shook, the insane laughter bubbling forth, along with gouts of blood.

Brandon could only watch horrified as the rogue with blood pouring from his eyes, mouth, nose, and ears convulsed to death.

Clint looked at the corpse dispassionately. "Well, that was a waste of time."

"What are we going to do?" asked Brandon, more shaken by the display than he would admit.

"Burn the body."

"I meant about whoever was mind-controlling the rogues?"

Clint's eyes glinted with steel, and his low answer echoed with menace. "Exactly what I said. Find him and kill him of course."

Chapter Ten

Back in his subterranean dwelling, the Master of the rogues snapped out of his trance. The loss of the dogs was regrettable but, in the long run, not important. He'd never truly expected them to beat the alpha, but he did enjoy the tendrils of wariness and fear the attack had spun. But forget the web of entrapment he wove. Of more interest and excitement was the discovery of the very thing he'd searched so long for. *I've found her.* The prize that had slipped his grasp so long ago but that, as the portents promised, had reappeared. Albeit in a different shape for him to claim.

She is here. His eager side, the impatient part of himself, wanted to order his minions to snatch her up right now. However, that simple solution skipped the fun and havoc that could, instead, pave the way to his ultimate victory. He'd seen the reaction of the head mongrel and his sidekick. *She's their mate. How much more entertaining it will be to tear her away from them, after waging a campaign of fear first of course.*

He did so enjoy watching the chaos he caused, the tendrils of dread he spun, binding his victims up in a web of fear until they became ripe for him to pluck.

Yes, if I orchestrate the next steps correctly, not only

will I acquire her but the head dogs will topple, giving me control of this city too.

And to think he owed it all to the magical tome he'd discovered so long ago. Years it had taken him to master the art of mind control painstakingly laid out step by step in the magical book. The power eventually became his, a fabulous ability that had evolved to the point that he could now force someone in his power to die, simply because he commanded it. His favorite pastime was the invasion of dreams, where he rooted out the sleeper's fears and then exploded them into a nightmare of entertaining proportions—for him at least.

What a pity a strong mind like the alpha's wouldn't succumb to his will. Perhaps, in time, he'd cultivate his abilities to overcome even the mightiest, turning them into his puppets. But if they refused to serve, then they could just bleed. *I will own this city.*

And with this as my base, I can spread the threads of my wicked web until none dare stand against me.

Chapter Eleven

Josie, lounging in pajamas, for the hour was still early, jumped when a knock sounded at her door. *Clint's here already?*

She bit her lip as she debated telling him to wait so she could run for a brush. Her usually bun-wrangled hair lay in unruly waves around her shoulders and drifted down her back. Her flustered state decided for her. *If he can't accept me with bed head, then I shouldn't even think of dating him.* Her dreams of the previous night had left her flushed, and she'd woken wanting, aroused, and no longer as caring if her heart was broken. She needed to become more daring, and allowing herself to enjoy Clint's attention was a good start. *I don't want to regret later on what could have been.*

Taking a deep breath, she flung open the door. A handful of flowers thrust at her was the first thing she saw, but she recognized the drawled good morning.

"Brandon?"

"Expecting someone else?" he joked, but the laughter in his eyes died a bit at her expression. "I see. Maybe I should leave."

"No. Please come in. I didn't properly thank you yesterday for making sure that wolf didn't get me. I've got coffee?" she cajoled when he hesitated.

He followed her in, shutting the door behind him. Josie went to her tiny kitchen, which opened onto the living room. Brandon wandered around, peering with curiosity at the contents of her crammed bookshelves. Josie found a vase for the flowers and set them out before she poured them coffee, which she knew, from the office, he took sweet and creamed.

She set the mugs on the breakfast bar and was about to call him when Snickers came flying out of nowhere and leapt onto Brandon's leg.

"What the fuck?" he exclaimed as her no-longer-so-docile kitty climbed up his leg, hissing and spitting.

Josie put a hand over her mouth so he wouldn't see the smile, for the scene was reminiscent of something off of *America's Funniest Home Videos.* "Um, that's my cat, Snickers. She, um, doesn't seem to like werewolves." *Now there's an understatement.*

Brandon, carefully unhooking the sharp claws, grimaced. "Gee, I'd have never guessed."

Annoyed that he was so put off by her pet's instinct, she muttered, "Like me, like my cat."

She'd thought she'd spoken low, but he still heard and answered her. "Hey, I'm prepared to love this cat if it means I get to be with its owner."

Josie blushed. "Your coffee's ready," she said, gesturing. He didn't sit down. Instead, he roamed some more, inspecting her few scattered pictures and even crouching to read the titles on her DVDs and CDs. Josie had never thought her apartment small until now. Somehow having a larger-than-life male invading it, one who, to her embarrassment, made her wet her panties as often as she did, made the space seem cozy.

She turned away from him, unable to understand how, given her attraction to Clint, she could even think of betraying their kiss from the previous eve with none other than his best friend. *Talk about wrong.*

Arms wrapped around her from behind, and Josie squeaked.

"What's wrong, honey?" Brandon asked before nuzzling her nape through her thick mane of hair.

A shiver went through her body, the sensation of his lips lightly brushing her skin too erotic for her to handle. "You shouldn't," she whispered.

He turned her in his arms, and he stared into her eyes with his warm brown ones, which melted her. "Why not?"

Josie fought his allure. "I, um, kind of kissed Clint. He's coming over later, so we really shouldn't . . ." She never got to finish her sentence because, instead of backing off, Brandon claimed her mouth with his, and her good intentions fled out the window.

Desire coiled in her cleft while heat spread its sensual tendrils throughout her. She'd been mistaken thinking only Clint could arouse her. Brandon held the power, too, and beneath the onslaught of his mouth, she couldn't think, but, oh, how she felt.

Big hands cupped her bottom, squeezing cheeks she'd always thought too plump, but he kneaded and weighed them with obvious enjoyment.

She squealed when her feet left the ground. He set her on the counter and inserted his body between her legs.

"You are so damned hot," he muttered, his eyes smoky. He kissed her again, and Josie melted, unable to resist his allure. Her fingers dug into his shoulders, and she panted into his mouth.

Knock. Knock. Knock.

The brisk thumping at her door made Brandon pull away with a mischievous grin. "I'll go see who's there," he said a little too gleefully, leaving Josie to recover her wits.

She slid off the counter on wobbly legs as the door opened on none other than Clint. If ever there was a moment she needed the ground to open up and swallow her, now was it.

I can't believe, not even twenty-four hours after I let Clint kiss me, I was making out with his best friend in my kitchen. I am a slut apparently and will surely burn in hell.

Josie tried to stand straight, a hard thing to do since she feared Clint's wrath. However, while Clint glared at Brandon's smug countenance, he was all smiles when he turned to her.

"Hey, baby," he said in greeting. "How'd you sleep?"

Incredulous that he wouldn't acknowledge the obvious fact that she'd been kissing Brandon, she, for some insane reason, brought it up. "How can you be so nonchalant? I was just kissing Brandon."

Clint shrugged. "But I kissed you first. Besides, it's who gets to kiss you last that counts."

Josie flushed, and anger slowly seeped into her. "So, let me get this straight. You're both pursuing me?" At their nods, her lips tightened. "Well, it's nice to know I'm nothing but a game between you guys."

"It's not like that," said Clint, holding out his hands, trying to look conciliatory.

"I think you both need to leave," she said, crossing her arms over her chest.

"But—" Brandon tried to speak, but she glared at him, and to her amazement, he folded under her stare.

She fought not to give in to the two ravishing men with matching puppy dog faces, a battle because they were so damned cute. After they had left, the murmur of their arguing voices came through the closed door.

Josie sighed and flopped onto her couch. "Great. I went from two men to no men. Now what are we going to do today?" Snickers, who'd hopped up beside her, just meowed.

With nothing else to do, Josie did laundry. *What a letdown.* Her building thankfully had a washer and dryer in the basement area, so, armed with a book and quarters, she lost herself in the world of romance as her clothes tumbled around in the machines. It was midafternoon when she finally emerged with her last load. She lugged it up the stairs to her apartment and balanced it on her hip as she unclipped her keys from her belt loop. A piece of paper fluttered in the jamb, and she let it fall to the floor when she opened the door. Only after she'd set her laundry down and closed the door did she pick up the hand-scrawled missive. In seconds, she was on the phone calling Clint with hands that shook.

Chapter Twelve

"How the hell did they find her?" ranted Brandon in the passenger seat of Clint's SUV.

"Did any of the rogues escape yesterday?"

"Did you seriously just ask me that?" Brandon shot him a dirty look.

"I'd say it's obvious then; we're being followed."

"By who, though?" growled Brandon. "And why threaten Josie?"

Clint's wolf bristled inside his skin. "I don't know, but they messed with the wrong pack if they think they can threaten our woman."

"Our woman?" said Brandon sardonically. "I'd say right now we're lucky she's even talking to us. She was really pissed this morning."

"And whose fault was that?" said Clint, glaring at Brandon.

"Hey, I went to check on her. I can't help wanting her. You, of all people, should know the feeling."

"Yeah," admitted Clint begrudgingly. "But now we've got to decide. Are we still going pursue her separately, or do we work together and tag-team?"

"I've always been a team player," quipped

Brandon. "And, besides, remember the fun we had with that blonde back in college?"

Clint did indeed. He hoped Josie wouldn't mind a seduction by two men. Then again, how could she resist when he and Brandon showed her how the love of two men would surpass her previous ideas of pleasure? Besides, with the danger she faced, he'd feel better knowing someone with the same emotional investment would also be watching her.

"Fine; that's settled easily enough, but now, how are we going to (A) get her to agree to it and (B) get her to move out to the ranch where we can keep her safe?"

"You forgot (C)," said Brandon with a twinkle in his eyes. "How do we convince her cat not to shred our manparts when we sleep?"

Clint chuckled. "I guess we'd better invest in some jockstraps because I doubt Josie will go anywhere without her furball."

"Maybe if I rub catnip all over me, her kitty will like me and get me back in her good graces," mused Brandon.

"Ha. I'm going with tuna myself."

They discussed ways of taming Josie's ferocious cat the rest of the drive, the silly banter not easing the anger still coursing through Clint, an anger that started when she'd called him in tears and probably wouldn't end until he killed the threat to his future mate.

She must have watched for them from the window, for she flung the door open as soon as they pulled out front with a screech. Her eyes were red, and her cheeks streaked with tears. She held her cat in her arms, which, as if sensing her mistress's need, only emitted a low growl in their direction.

"Where's the note?" asked Clint. She pointed behind her, her expression so frail Clint braved the claws of her cat to wrap his arms around her. She shuddered in his embrace, and the cat, with a squawk, struggled loose. Clint watched over her head as Brandon spotted the note on the living room table and snatched it up to read. His beta's face lost its usual joviality, and his eyes turned flinty.

It must be nasty for Brandon not to joke about it.

Brandon spun an unresisting Josie into his arms, handing Clint the note in the process.

Don't think your testosterone-laden dogs will stop me when I come for you. Your time is fast approaching, and I will allow nothing to stand in my way. Tell your puppies if they know what's good for them, they'll roll over and prepare to greet their new master.

Rage—and icy fear for Josie—coursed through him. Marked or not, Josie was his. The thought of harm coming to her made his wolf howl in his mind and push to come to the surface, eager to hunt down the one who thought to threaten what was theirs. Instead of giving voice to all this, Clint simply said, "You're moving."

Josie pushed out of Brandon's arms and looked between them. "Move? Isn't that a bit extreme?"

"This note is no joke, Josie. The people in our world don't play by the rules, you know. They've discerned you're important to us, and they'll hurt you to get to us," Clint replied. He didn't mention that anyone who harmed a single strand of hair on her head would not survive his wrath.

"I'm important?" Her voice, vulnerable along with her bright eyes, made him groan, and he crushed her to him. Actually, she ended up sandwiched as Brandon hugged her from the back.

"Baby, I can't explain it right now, but trust me when I say Brandon and I would rather die than see one hair on your head harmed."

"Fine. Let's say I believe you. Where is it you want me to move and for how long?"

Clint didn't say forever, even as he thought it. "We'll move you out to the ranch until we've taken care of the danger to you. I've got plenty of spare rooms." *And a really large bed.* "I can also get a couple of the pack to patrol the grounds and prevent any unwelcome visitors."

"What about my place and Snickers?"

Clint looked at her blankly for a second until he realized she meant the cat and not the chocolate bar. "We'll bring your cat, of course, and if you don't mind, I'd like to station a pair of my guys here to keep an eye out."

She bit her lower lip, and her glance bounced between him and Brandon. Finally, with a sigh, she nodded her head. "Fine. I'll come. Just give me a few minutes to pack a bag. I'll also need to grab the cat carrier from my storage unit in the basement."

She left them to go to her bedroom, and Brandon turned to Clint, his eyes furious. "What the fuck is going on? First, this asshole sends some rogues at us, and then he threatens Josie. I want to find this son of a bitch and take him apart."

Clint smiled, but his eyes remained flinty.

"Oh, we'll find him and make him regret even thinking of harming our little mouse. But on a bright note, we'll have Josie with us at the ranch, where she belongs."

Brandon grinned. "Are we flipping to see who gets to sleep with her first, under the guise of guarding of course?"

"My house, my turn first."

Brandon would have retorted, but Josie was back lugging a knapsack. Clint raised an eyebrow in surprise. *She's certainly not like other women and their stacks of luggage.* Not that she'd need many clothes if he had his way. He'd prefer she get naked and stayed that way.

Wrangling the cat into the cage proved interesting, and Josie had several scratches before Clint bent down and let out a menacing growl. The cat took one look at him and, with a disdainful sniff, turned to march into the cage.

Damned felines. Another problem solved, the trio made its way to Clint's SUV, where he gnashed his teeth as he realized that, by driving, he'd placed Josie in the back seat with Brandon.

Josie, as if realizing this, finagled it so that Brandon sat in front on the passenger side while she rode in the row behind with her cat.

Clint smirked at Brandon, who scowled. Despite the fact that they'd agreed to share her, it didn't mean healthy competition wasn't alive and flourishing.

Halfway across town, Clint heard the question he'd dreaded.

"Why are we going this way? I thought you

said I was on your way to work."

A deep laugh emerged from Brandon. "You are on the way if we take a scenic twenty-minute detour."

"I wouldn't talk, seeing as how you also had to detour," said Clint with a scowl.

Josie giggled. "You guys are too much. Are you always this competitive?"

"Yes."

"No."

Josie let out peals of laughter, some of it, Clint suspected, pent-up hysteria from her now-dissipated fear.

"So, where do you live?" she finally asked.

"You'll see," replied Clint enigmatically. He wanted to see her reaction firsthand when she saw his place.

Only once they'd left the trappings of the city behind did he turn onto a gravel road, the long drive winding through dense trees until it emerged in a bright clearing where the ranch sat.

She gasped. "Oh, Clint, it's gorgeous."

Clint's chest puffed up with pride. "It's been in the family for several generations, but my dad wasn't into updating much. So, when I inherited, I gave it a major overhaul."

"Is all this land yours, too?" she asked, her nose pressed to the window as she peered at the lush greenery that surrounded the ranch house, from cleared lawns to a vast garden bordered by dense brush and trees.

"Yup. Over thirty-five acres." Clint pulled up in front of the house, and Brandon bounded out of the SUV and opened the door for Josie to step out. Lucky him, he was stuck carrying the cat carrier with the very pissed-off feline. But it wasn't all bad. He got to admire the view of Josie's ass as she walked up the steps and entered his home. *Our home now, baby.*

Chapter Thirteen

Josie peeked around with interest. The house from outside appeared like an *L*-shaped bungalow. Inside, it was huge and open. To the right of the vestibule was a massive living room with a floor-to-ceiling stone fireplace. There had to be a half-dozen couches scattered around, along with an equal number of chairs. The floors made of wide-planked wood gleamed, their lacquered surface covered here and there with bright, rag-woven rugs. Her inspection temporarily halted at the sound of Snickers' meow of unhappiness.

Josie dropped to her knees and sweet-talked Snickers as she unlatched the cage. "Now you be a good girl. No clawing anything, and that means the werewolves too, not just the furniture." Snickers, of course, didn't reply and bolted as soon as the door opened on the cage. Josie hoped she didn't get into too much trouble.

Standing back up, she caught Clint's grin. However, it was Brandon who spoke. "Promise me you'll never baby-talk me when I'm a wolf. I'd never live down the ridicule."

Josie smirked. "Oh, but weren't you the pretty blond wolf? Don't worry. I won't just baby-talk you. I'll probably scratch you behind the ears, too."

Clint roared with laughter at Brandon's face until Josie added, "You, too, big guy."

Josie left them both staring at each other. The rich sound of masculine chuckles—which had her shivering in naughty places—accompanied her as she walked farther into the house. She traversed the long length of the living room to encounter the world's biggest freaking kitchen.

"Good grief. This place is big enough to feed an army," she exclaimed.

"Or a pack of hungry wolves," said Clint with a wolfish grin as he walked by her to open the fridge. "Speaking of which, I could use some dinner. How about you, baby?"

"I'd love to see you cook." Josie blushed at her words, hearing the double meaning, which Clint also caught. Instead of replying, he just winked at her. Josie couldn't help the heat that pooled between her thighs. *The man is just too darned good-looking for his own good.*

Josie seated herself at a stool that bordered the massive granite-topped island, and Brandon perched himself beside her.

As Clint proved he did know his way around a kitchen and the massive stove with eight burners, she started assuaging her curiosity. "So, I take it you're boss of the werewolves. How many are in your pack?" Her usual timidity had evaporated around Clint and Brandon. It was hard to be scared of two guys who kissed her as if she was the only girl in the world and dropped everything to protect her.

"My proper title is alpha, and Brandon here is my beta. We've got a moderate-sized group, compared to others, at thirty-seven. Of course, there's about a dozen of the pack out right now on transport runs. You've actually met almost all of them at this point, seeing as how they pretty much all work for the company."

"Wait, back up a second. Did I understand you correctly? You mean there's other werewolf packs out there, too?"

"There are hundreds of packs. Each major territory has at least one. They're not all wolves, though. Shifters run a gamut of animals like bears, big cats, reptiles, and more. And that's just the most prolific groups. Some species don't have enough numbers to form packs, like the dragons."

Josie's eyes grew wider. "You're screwing with me, aren't you? I mean, dragons. Seriously?"

"Hell yeah, dragons," Brandon said, jumping in with a grin. "Actually, you'll probably end up meeting one soon, as Draco is due for a visit in the next month or so. And if you think that's messed-up, there are also dolphin packs, and I've even heard of a spider shifter running around."

Josie shuddered. "A man-sized spider? That is so gross." *And like my nightmare.*

Clint frowned at Brandon. "Don't worry. The rules all of our kind abide by state that all shifters must present themselves to the alpha if they intend to spend any time in a controlled territory."

"So, you knew those wolves that attacked you?"

Clint shook his head. "Those were rogues. In other words, shifters who weren't obeying pack laws and thus were subject to justice."

"That's nuts, though. What did they expect to accomplish?"

Clint shrugged and kept silent. He finished flipping the thick ham steaks and threw them on some plates, along with a salad and some pan-fried rice.

Josie dug in, hungrier than she expected, but she still had questions. "Do you have female werewolves, too?"

"Yes, but they are much rarer. The shifter gene transfers better in males, which is why many of our females have more than one mate." However, while it was quite common for female shifters to take on multiple mates, it was a lot rarer for a human to attract the attention of more than one male. Clint assumed it had to do with the fragile nature of most humans.

"Two?"

Brandon chuckled. "Or more. Don't tell me you've never fantasized about it?"

Josie blushed and dropped her head. She tried changing the subject. "I guess you and Brandon haven't found your mates yet?"

"Oh, we have," said Clint huskily.

Irrational jealousy made her meet his eyes. "And she's okay with you kissing other women and bringing them into your home?" Josie couldn't believe she blurted that out loud.

"You tell me," he retorted.

What? Josie looked at him blankly, not understanding, but when the lightbulb went off—*oh my god, I think he's talking about me*—she ducked her head again. She kept quiet after that, finishing her meal as she mulled over what she'd learned, even more confused than before. *If I didn't know better, I'd think he implied I am his mate. But that's impossible because I'm not a werewolf.*

She helped Clint stack the dishes in the washer while Brandon started a fire in the hearth. There was one couch facing the dancing flames, and when Clint and Brandon took a seat at either end, she debated sitting in the middle, but her nervousness returned, and she, instead, knelt on the rug with her back to them.

Their synchronized chuckle sent shivers down her spine, and moisture formed in her cleft. Even though she'd found herself alone with them since their departure of her place, she now noticed just how alone they were. *Me, my absent cat, and two big, bad wolves.* It was a recipe for pleasure, if she could find the courage to take what they offered.

"Baby," whispered Clint's voice right beside her ear. She jumped, for she hadn't heard him move. "Why are you fighting it? We can smell your desire."

Josie wrinkled her nose as she blushed. "That's kind of gross."

Brandon's soft laughter fluttered her hair around her other ear. *Someone should put bells on them so I can hear them coming.*

"Little mouse, the things we want to do with you are far from gross, but they might be sticky, hot, and, I promise you, pleasurable."

"I don't understand what you want from me," she blurted out, unable to look them in the face and even more unable to stop the heat from spreading throughout her body.

"We want you," answered Clint.

"By *we*, I assume you want to share me? Swap me back and forth like some trading card?"

"Well, we could take turns, I guess," said Brandon, nuzzling her lobe. "But wouldn't it be more fun if we both took care of you at once?"

Unbidden, an image of both men, touching her, pleasing her at the same time, arose in her mind. Her breath caught, and she could not stop the blush that burned her skin nor the moisture that slicked her cleft.

Clint trailed kisses along her jaw. "Haven't you figured it out yet? Human or not, you're our mate, and we want you."

"What does that mean?" she asked, her voice high-pitched as she fought the pleasurable sensations.

"We want to mark you, claim you as ours."

"You mean bite?" she squeaked.

"Just a little nibble. We'd be in human form," Clint said to reassure her. "There'd be no danger to your humanity."

"But won't it hurt?" Josie couldn't believe they were even having the conversation. *Welcome to the twilight zone, where hunky men are werewolves who want to bite you and claim you as mate.*

Brandon purred in her ear. "By the time we bite you, you'll be riding our cocks, caught in the throes of the most intense orgasm you've ever experienced."

Josie's breath caught in her throat as he vocalized her fantasy of a moment ago. *Did he read my mind?* "But . . ." The protest in her mouth died. Actually, it was captured by Clint's mouth. While he caressed her parted lips, Brandon stroked the sensitive flesh behind her ear with his tongue. As sensual assaults went, she surrendered with their first attack.

She didn't protest when they laid her down on the carpet. On either side, their male bodies pressed against her, the hardness of their desire poking into her sides. Josie kept her hands to herself, overwhelmed and unsure what she should do.

Her body knew what it wanted, though, and it arched of its own volition. A pair of hands, each large but different in texture, found their way up her shirt and squeezed her breasts. Josie gasped as they popped her globes free from her restricting bra and stroked callused thumbs over the tips, which burgeoned into erect points.

A thick thigh inserted itself between her legs, and she wantonly rubbed her covered sex against it, the friction of the cloth separating still serving to heighten her arousal. The fabric of her shirt was pushed up, and a hot mouth latched onto her nipple. The sucking sensation, intense and jolting her aching cleft, made her cry out.

She wanted to open her eyes to watch, but the decadence of having two men pleasuring her kept them closed. A hand slid down to the front of her slacks, the material stretching just enough to accommodate the exploring hand. The brush of fingers across the damp material of her panties made her shudder.

"Oh, please," she breathed, the begging words rising unbidden. They answered her wanton cry. Her damp, cotton panties were pushed aside to allow access to a finger. Slowly, the callused tip rubbed over her sensitized clit, drawing mewling cries from her.

The mouth devouring her breast kept up its sensual work, flicking and nipping at her engorged bud in time to the hand down her pants that stroked her wet folds. When the damp digits pushed into her, she let out a moan as her pelvic muscles clenched tight, her orgasm just a thrust or two away.

A clearing throat with a muttered, "sorry to bother," found her abruptly hand- and mouth-free. Josie opened her bleary, passion-glazed eyes to see both Clint and Brandon kneeling on one side of her, hiding her partially nude body from view.

Caught in a compromising situation, with not one but two men, Josie scrambled, mortified, to a seated position and righted her clothes. She didn't pay attention to the low-timbered conversation until the end when she heard the words, "We'll have to get a cleaner in to clean up the blood and fix the window at her place."

Are they talking about my apartment? "What happened?" she interjected.

Brandon didn't answer her question as he turned to give her a hand to help her stand.

"Take care of Josie while I go check this out," ordered Clint. His bright eyes gazed on her with longing, and he turned to walk away, only to whirl right back. He grabbed Josie around the waist and gave her a hard kiss. "Don't worry, baby. You're safe here."

With those words, he did leave with Ralph, whom she recognized from work. Brandon slid an arm around her waist and guided her out of the living room—and away from her embarrassment. *What was I thinking? Making love to two men at once and out in the open. Oh my God, I can just imagine the rumors and snickers I'll have to endure at work.*

Once again, Brandon read her thoughts. "It's not a big deal."

"Says you," she muttered darkly. "It's different for men."

"It's different in packs," he corrected. "Like we said before, it's not uncommon for one woman to attract the attention of two or more men."

"I'm human, remember? It seems strange to me."

"Well, you'd better get used to the idea because, my dear little mouse, you will be mated to Clint and me."

"What if I don't want to?" She acted contrary, even as her body—and heart—screamed *yes.*

Brandon halted their progress up the hall and pinned her to the wall. "Don't challenge me to prove you wrong," he said, his mouth hovering close to hers.

"Everything's happening so fast. I mean first I find out you're werewolves. Then someone threatens me. And now you expect me to just swallow the fact that you and Clint intend to bite me and…and be intimate with me at the same time." She couldn't say it without blushing.

"You can't tell me you don't feel the same pull, the need to touch us, skin to skin."

"Great, I'm a magnet for werewolves," she grumbled.

"Only two," he replied.

"And here I thought you liked me for me."

His brown eyes gazed down at her, and he smiled gently. "What's the difference? Some men are attracted by looks, others intelligence, and then there's the ones who see a woman and instantly feel a connection. Does the root cause matter?"

Does it? "If it weren't for this pull, you would never have looked at me twice."

"Don't be so sure," he murmured, dipping his head down. "There are many things about you that I enjoy, Josie."

His lips skimmed hers, reigniting the fire that, while banked at the interruption, still simmered beneath the surface.

Brandon broke the kiss before it went too far. "I'm needed outside. Stay inside where it's safe."

"When will you be back?"

"Soon. Why, did you want me to join you in bed later?"

A part of Josie—the wanton side—screamed 'Yes!', but her meek side couldn't bring itself to voice it aloud. That and she needed to think more on what they wanted from her and decide if she could handle it emotionally *because physically my body is all for it. It's my heart I'm worried about.*

Her answer must have shown in her face, for humor lit his eyes, and he brushed his knuckles across her cheek. "When you're ready, we'll be here for you. Dream of us."

He walked away, and Josie bit her lower lip as she watched the sexy waggle of his ass receding.

I am such a ninny. Why did I say no?

Maybe because the one thing they'd both never said was what happened after the threesome and biting. Would they go on their merry way when they tired of her, breaking her heart?

Or, even scarier, would they want a forever-after? *Hey, Dad, can you make two extra spots for Christmas dinner because I'm bringing home not one but two boyfriends?*

Despite the awkwardness involved in explaining a polygamous relationship to friends and family, she couldn't deny she was intrigued. *Who am I trying to kid? I'm already in love with them both. So, why am I fighting the perfect solution?* Her mind knew the answer. Because they'd never said they loved her.

Given a room, with her things already placed in it, Josie readied herself for sleep then tossed and turned in the strange bed, her mind in turmoil as she tried to decide the best course for her. As night deepened, she almost regretted not taking Brandon up on his offer of a bedmate. It even occurred to her to search him or Clint out. She didn't want to close her eyes, for she sensed the tendrils of fear reaching out to snare her. Her nightmare was just waiting for her to fall asleep. Like a dark predator, it hid in the corners of her mind, waiting for a moment when her guard was lowered. She fought against slumber, fought the drag that pulled her eyelids down. But fatigue won and tugged her into its chilling maw. Within moments, she was screaming—just not out loud.

Chapter Fourteen

Clint couldn't sleep, not knowing Josie was only a room away. This whole taking-it-slow thing was really chafing, but Josie was the type to flee if she felt cornered. So, against his desires, and to the chagrin of his raging hard-on, he lay on his bed, hands laced under his head, planning the next step in his seduction.

The scene out at her apartment had chilled him, for he realized if they hadn't come to rescue her, it might very well have been her blood decorating the carpet and walls in her place. As it was, the two pack members he'd left to guard her place were in bad shape. They'd heal, but whatever attacked them had been vicious, and even more disturbing, neither victim remembered a thing. Their foe appeared to not only be some kind of mind-fucker he was also wily. The eye-watering fumes and overwhelming stench of ammonia splashed about the apartment foiled their attempts to track by scent. *What the fuck are we dealing with?*

When he'd arrived back at the ranch, dreading Brandon's triumphant grin—for in his place he would have seduced his sweet Josie—he found himself happy that Brandon hadn't gotten lucky while he was out. A possible perimeter breach had sent Brandon outside to check on things, and while a false alarm, he hadn't the chance to pursue a lone seduction of Josie.

And, as Brandon grimly informed Clint, she'd refused the offer of nighttime company. Probably a smart move on her part, given he didn't think he'd have resisted the seductive allure of her body for platonic rest. It was the reason why he hadn't sneaked into her room to cuddle her in repose. Had she woken, he would have claimed it was for protection, but in honesty, he just didn't like being apart from her. So, instead of spooning and making love to his woman, he stared at the ceiling in his room with a hard-on to batter down doors.

The blood in his veins froze as he heard, with acute auditory senses, Josie whimper through the walls. Unease gripped him. In a flash, he was out in the hall with his hand on her doorknob. A prickling sensation at his back let him know Brandon had joined him. They might not have marked her, but the connection, even if faint, was there between them.

Together, they proceeded with caution into her room. It was pitch-black, but to a shifter, that meant nothing. Their enhanced nature allowed them to see in the dark—the tool of a predator that hunts at night. The room, to his relief, contained no intruders, only a thrashing Josie, and yet, there was a scent in the air that didn't belong. Clint inhaled the musty aroma and almost gagged at the alien stench.

"What is that smell?" whispered Brandon.

"I don't know," muttered Clint, "but I do believe that Josie's nightmares aren't a product of her mind but someone else's." Even as he spoke, Josie let out a shriek, a chilling cry that was suddenly muffled as if someone had gagged her. Brandon flicked on the bedroom light, dispelling the shadows as Clint dove onto the bed next to a catatonic Josie, looking for a foe that didn't exist for him to fight. Frustration made him curse as he beheld her, helpless. Her eyes stared ahead of her, glazed with terror and unseeing when he waved his hand in front of her. Brandon, on her other side, touched her hand, but he quickly snatched it back. He shook it.

"What the fuck? She's ice-cold!" Brandon said.

"Something's screwing with her dreams. We've got to snap her out of it." Clint tried shouting and shaking her pajama-clad shoulders, but she remained caught in the unnatural nightmare. Clint let out a sound of vexation, for he couldn't fight something he couldn't touch.

Brandon looked just as lost. *But we can't give up. She needs us.* Clint straddled Josie and placed his face directly in front of her unseeing eyes. "Josie, baby, I need you to wake up." He hadn't expected her to respond. Not knowing what else to do, Clint did the only thing he could think of to jolt her body. He kissed her.

Her lips were so cold it was like embracing a corpse, but at the skin-to-skin contact, she let out a small gasp. Encouraged, he slanted his lips across hers again and was rewarded with them warming under his touch.

"She needs skin-to-skin contact," said Clint, removing his lips only long enough to inform Brandon.

“I’m all for that,” said Brandon. “Here, lift up a bit so I can pull down the covers. The more of her skin we touch, the better.”

Clint leaned up to aid Brandon in pulling down the sheets, all the while keeping his lips locked to hers. Brandon didn’t stop at the sheets, though. He tugged her top up and her bottoms down, leaving her cool skin exposed. Clint shifted to the side and pressed his bare chest against her cold ribs while Brandon did the same on her other side.

Slowly, her body warmed to their touch, and her lips parted with a sigh under his. Brandon, for his part, was sliding his lips from hers down to the tip of her breast then around again. Her skin lost its pallor, and when Brandon clamped his mouth down over her breast and she arched, Clint knew they were winning.

He watched her face as he continued to kiss her, his tongue pushing inside her mouth to slide along hers. Her eyes went from catatonic to aware in moments.

“Welcome back, baby,” he murmured.

Chapter Fifteen

Josie snapped out of her nightmare into bliss. The chill of her nighttime ordeal fled under the onslaught of two mouths determined to draw a response from her body—with erotic success. The chains of her nightmare broken, she responded with an ardor she'd never have thought possible, her qualms forgotten in the building warmth and pleasure. *Who cares about the future? I need to start finding the bravery to live life to the fullest, starting with now.*

"Let us love you, baby," murmured Clint against her mouth before slipping his tongue back between her lips. Josie replied by kissing him back with all the passion she felt thrumming through her.

Clint's wasn't the only busy mouth. A second set of lips, belonging to Brandon, were busy kissing the soft skin under her ear. He flicked his tongue against the curl of her lobe. "So glad you decided to join us," Brandon said with a wicked chuckle as he moved down her body to tease her erect buds.

Josie arched on the bed at the feel of his mouth on her taut nipple. Clint's lips left hers, and she mourned their loss until she divined the direction of his mouth. Down her body he moved, his firm lips nipping and gliding across her smooth skin and over the swell of her abdomen to her curls. She trembled from head to toe as his mouth hovered so close to her most intimate spot. He blew on her softly, his breath warm and promising.

Her sex quivered, and she could feel the moisture pooling, waiting for his touch. But he tortured her, kissing the soft skin of her inner thigh. Licking his way around the edges of her nether lips. Brushing his mouth across her sensitized nub.

"Please," she whimpered, her need stronger than her shyness.

He placed his mouth on her sex, his hot tongue flicking her clit, and Josie bucked off the bed with a cry. A body—a very naked one—straddled her as she opened her eyes to see Brandon, his eyes alit with passion, staring down at her. With a sensual smile, he caught her hands and held them above her head, stretching her body and trapping her.

Clint's mouth returned to her pussy, and fire raced through her. Restrained, she couldn't thrash or relieve the incredible pleasure that swept over her like a tidal wave. It took only moments for it to become too much. With a piercing scream, she came, the force of her orgasm intense enough that she couldn't see for a moment.

Brandon moved off her, and she turned her head to watch him as he knelt beside her on the bed, his hand stroking his erect cock. So mesmerized was she by the motion of his hand sliding up and down his shaft she didn't see Clint poise himself between her thighs. With her breathing still hard and her channel quivering with aftershocks, Clint sheathed himself.

"Oh dear God," she muttered, her eyes

almost rolling back in her head at the sensation.

"Damn, baby, you feel so freaking good," grunted Clint as he stroked in and out of her. His heavy body glistened with perspiration, and his hands pushed her legs up to rest on his shoulders, seating him even deeper inside.

Josie mewled and clawed at the sheets as the head of his cock bumped a sensitive spot inside. Again and again, he ground against the unseen pleasure button while Josie could only thrash her head at the rapture he wrung from her body.

"I can't hold on," groaned Clint, who thrust one last time in her body and held himself rigid as his shaft spurted hotly inside her.

Josie mewled in complaint when he withdrew but not for long, as Brandon switched spots with Clint and took over.

Where Clint's cock was thick, Brandon's was longer and slightly curved. He pumped into her, his cock unerringly striking her sweet spot each time, and already at the pinnacle, Josie climaxed again, her whimpering cries caught by Clint's mouth as he kissed her.

She assumed Brandon came, but she didn't actually perceive it. She did know her body had never felt more sated. *And I've never felt sexier, more womanly.*

The old Josie would have worried what to do when fantastic sex with two men finished. The new Josie, who'd just discovered two was better than one, just curled against the side of one and waggled her bottom against the one that spooned her back.

Cuddled between them, more content than she ever remembered feeling, she fell into a dreamless sleep.

Chapter Sixteen

Waking up sandwiched between two men was a blushing experience, especially when she had to extricate herself to take care of nature. She foolishly thought she'd managed it without waking them until she sauntered across the room naked and she heard a low wolf whistle.

Blushing, she dashed the rest of the way to the bathroom and slammed the door. She took care of business and brushed her teeth. While she automatically ran through her routine of morning necessities, she looked at herself in the mirror. *How strange; I look the same.*

Somehow, she'd thought sleeping with two men—especially werewolf ones—would have left a mark on her or shown itself. However, other than plump red lips, bright eyes, and a few chafe marks on her smooth skin, she looked like she always did, even if she felt like a whole new woman.

When she remembered the pleasure of the night, her lips curled into a smile and her nipples puckered. In the mirror, she marveled as she saw the transformation. Timid Josie disappeared, and in her place stood a seductress. *And wow, I am hot.*

She almost gathered up enough courage to saunter out naked again, but modesty—and shyness—prevailed, and she wrapped a large towel around herself before exiting the bathroom.

Only Brandon remained in bed, the sheet drawn up to his waist, leaving his chest, naked and muscled—*oh my*—exposed to her hungry view. He'd laced his hands behind his head, and he grinned at her perusal for, while she'd enjoyed a fleeting glimpse of his body before, in the light of day and without the adrenaline of the previous time, it ended up quite a different matter.

"Morning," she murmured, her dreaded cowardly nature making her duck her eyes.

"Don't you dare get all bashful on us again," he admonished. "I know what a wildcat you are now. So, unless you want me to prove what a hellion in bed you are, stand up straight."

Josie couldn't help the smile at the tart rejoinder. "What if I'd prefer you prove it to me again?" Her eyes met his with a mischievous twinkle. With a growl he came bounding out of bed, six foot something of blond hunk. And, instead of running like her timid side shouted, she dropped her towel.

Brandon's shocked eyes locked on her nude form, and he stumbled. The look of disbelief on his face as he hit the floor made her laugh until a slap on her bare bottom made her yelp.

She whirled to see Clint with eyes that twinkled. "What's so funny?" asked Clint, wrapping his arms around her, squishing her naked form to his only partially clad one. His bare chest rubbed against hers, and her nipples hardened.

"My two left feet apparently," grumbled Brandon, moving in to hug her from behind. The press of so much skin against hers woke a hunger in her that had nothing to do with food. *I wonder when I'll get a turn to taste them.* Her cheeks burned at the direction of her naughty thoughts that moistened her cleft.

Clint's eyes smoldered as if he knew. "Morning, baby," he murmured, dropping a kiss on the tip of her nose.

"Hi," she replied, tongue-tied but not because of bashfulness. It had more to do with the close proximity of the two male bodies and the arousal they inspired. "So, what's for breakfast?" she asked, sniffing some bacon wafting through the open door.

"How's sausage sound?" replied Clint.

Brandon snorted. "I think she might prefer it if we shower before we feed her those."

Josie blushed while Clint scowled. "I meant breakfast sausage. Along with bacon, eggs, and some toast. Josie needs to eat if she's going to keep up with us," he said with a soft smile for her alone.

"Um, I don't suppose I could get dressed first?" she queried.

"If you insist." Clint sighed. "But make them easy access," he said with a leer.

Josie laughed as she shooed them out the door and dressed. It occurred to her to let them watch, but she knew where that would have ended up. And she truly needed food and a shower before she romped again.

However, romp with them she would, even if it still made her blush. *One taste and I'm hooked.*

Chapter Seventeen

Brandon just threw on a pair of pants and met with Clint in the kitchen as they waited for Josie to eat breakfast. Keeping an eye and ear on the door, he spoke in a low voice to Clint.

"What the fuck happened last night? That was no normal dream."

"No it wasn't," agreed Clint grimly. "And from what she's told me, she's had those nightmares a while. Although I don't think they're nightmares so much as someone messing with her mind."

"We need to find the bastard who's messing with her head and take care of him. I won't stand for someone hurting our little mouse."

"More like lioness. Jeez, I knew she hid some passion under her meek exterior, but damn, I didn't expect a volcano."

Brandon grinned. "Yeah, that was a nice surprise. So, when do we introduce her to what having two men really entails, and a better question, when do we mark her? My wolf's damn near going ballistic in my head with wanting her."

"I know what you mean. I came damn near to losing control last night. It's why I came so fast. It was that or bite her without her permission. But we've got to be careful. She's come around quicker than I would have expected. I'm beginning to think that part of her meekness comes from the nightmare. It's a wonder she can even function with that kind of shit happening to her when she sleeps."

Brandon sighed. "So much for spending the day in bed. We need to take care of this, don't we?"

Clint nodded, not looking happy at the prospect either. "Think we can convince her to hang out here for the day while we do some scouting?"

"We'll promise her a sweet treat for later," Brandon replied. They were both chuckling when Josie walked into the kitchen and eyed them suspiciously.

"I'm afraid to ask what's so funny."

"Listen, after breakfast, Clint and I need to take care of some business. We'll leave guards, though, so you'll be safe here while you bathe and stuff. Although I'd recommend a nap for what we have planned for tonight."

Josie blushed, a trait he hoped she never lost because he found it so damned cute. "I don't need a nap. And besides, I've got to get to work. I'm late as it is already."

"No work," Clint said with a frown. "The warehouse isn't secure enough."

"Do you really think I'm in that much danger?" Josie lost her smile, and her features looked pale.

Brandon cursed. "Just a precaution, little mouse. If you feel a need to be productive, then you can work off Clint's computer in his office. I'm sure if you feel a need to bark some order, you can always call and ask them to put you on speaker phone."

"I don't bark," she muttered. "I ensure efficiency."

"Call it what you want, baby. Please, just stay here where it's safe for our peace of mind." Clint's eyes pleaded with hers.

"You won't be doing anything dangerous?" she asked, chewing her lower lip with worry.

"Us?" said Brandon with wide-eyed innocence.

Josie snorted, and Brandon continued to tease her until she'd lost her wan look and was giggling.

When they went to depart, the bleak expression was back in her eyes. Clint kissed her first, a fierce embrace that left her flushed and panting. Brandon spun her from his friend's arms into his. He also kissed her breathless, his nose twitching at the scent of her arousal, the sweetest perfume he'd ever enjoyed.

Don't worry, little mouse. Once we take care of the menace after you, we'll take care of all your needs. Forever.

Chapter Eighteen

Josie tried working and managed to lose herself in it for a few hours, but by late afternoon, she was pacing. *Why aren't they back yet? I know they're not at the office, and since the guards they left just shrug when I ask, I can guess, whatever it is they're up to, it's dangerous. It probably has to do with the note I got and the attack on my place.*

She still couldn't understand why anyone would want to hurt her. She was a no one. The only thing she could think of was she'd gotten caught into some kind of pack struggle and the perpetrators thought that, by hurting her, they'd hurt Clint and Brandon. Silly, of course. Just because they'd slept with her didn't mean they cared any further, even if they kept hinting.

And what if it's not a joke? Can I handle being in a committed relationship with two men, two men that turn furry, that is? Just fantasizing about staying with them, loving them—for, despite herself, her heart was caught up in it all—made her think of something chilling. *What if I get pregnant? Oh my God. We didn't use any protection. What if I already am?*

The thought didn't terrify her. Actually, a warm glow suffused her at the thought of two babies, one with a dark mop and the other with a golden one. But was that what the guys wanted, or was she projecting her own fantasies on things they'd implied? *I need to remember that just because they want to bite me and make me their mate because of some instinct doesn't mean they love me. I guess it boils down to, knowing that I love them, can I handle it if they don't?*

A knock on the door snapped her out of her endless circling of the question, and she went to answer. A disheveled guard named Bryant stood in the doorway.

His ball cap hung low over his face, and with the sun setting at his back, his features were indistinct, but his eyes shone bright, and Josie flinched back.

"Sorry to startle you, ma'am," he said in a soothing tone. "But it would seem your cat somehow got out of the house and is stuck up a tree."

"Snickers escaped?" Immediately concerned for her cat, Josie stuck her feet into her shoes to follow Bryant out of the house and off the porch. "Where is she?"

"If you'll follow me, I'll take you to her." Bryant took off at a brisk walk, and Josie followed, glancing back at the house and wondering if she should have left a note. *That's silly. I'll be back in a minute, and besides, I'm safe with Clint's guard.*

They walked farther than she expected, right to the edge of the woods bordering the cleared area for the house. Twilight lengthened the shadows, which, in turn, tightened her nerves, and dread coiled in her stomach. She was just about to ask Bryant if he was sure about where they were going when she heard the meow from up ahead.

"Snickers!" she called. "I'm here, kitty. Come see your mama." Josie passed Bryant and headed toward the brush that bordered the treeline.

Meow. Meow. The plaintive sound echoed from the woods, and Josie, feeling that Bryant was following a few paces back, swallowed her fear, even as her knees knocked. *I can do this. It's just some trees. They can't hurt me. And Snickers won't come to a werewolf.*

Thoughts of her poor kitty moved her feet forward, even as fear chilled her skin.

Meow.

The sound came from just in front of her. Josie stepped forward. "Snickers. Where are you, kitty?"

But instead of finding her cat, she came face to face with a stranger. She whirled, meaning to hide behind Bryant, but he stood right behind her, a twisted smile on his face.

"Bryant?" she questioned tentatively.

A low chuckle emerged, a slimy sound that made her skin pimple. "Bryant's no longer home. But soon you will be in my home, where you belong."

"No," Josie shouted, and she dodged to run around Bryant who was no longer Bryant. Like an idiot, she'd forgotten the stranger behind her. She made it one step before she was tackled to the ground. She found the courage to kick and bite, but when she managed a scream, a sound quickly cut off, she felt a prick in her arm.

The world spun, and through bleary eyes, she watched the ground moving as one of them slung her over a shoulder and traipsed through the woods to a car parked on the verge.

The inside of the trunk proved spacious, enough for her captor to dump her within. The effects of the injected drug took effect. The last thing that ran through her mind before she lost consciousness was, *Help me, please.*

Chapter Nineteen

Clint cursed as yet another promising lead—an interesting scent for his wolf—led to a dead end. Whoever controlled the rogues and threatened Josie had hidden their tracks well. He had wolves spread throughout the city; they listened to rumors and followed their noses as they checked for new smells.

But a whole day of searching ended up in a pile of squat. Well, not entirely. One of their ranks had accidentally come across his mate and was now off celebrating, naked in bed, which was where Clint wished he was now, Josie at his side.

Clint clambered back into his SUV, Brandon seating himself on the passenger side.

"So, now what, boss?" Brandon asked, his tone just as weary.

"I don't know. I think it's time to call it a day," said Clint, frustration evident in his tone. "We're not getting anywhere searching blindly. Maybe we need to change tactics."

"What do you mean?" asked Brandon, leaning back in his seat and closing his eyes.

"Right now we're looking for a needle in a haystack. What we need is a magnet."

Brandon shot up in his seat. "No way. You can't seriously be thinking of using Josie as bait. She could get hurt!"

Clint slapped the steering wheel. "I'm aware of the danger, but what other choice do we have? Whoever is fucking with us is laughing right now as we run around in circles chasing our own tails. Not to mention, we're spreading ourselves thin and tiring the pack."

"I don't like it. We've only been at it a day. I'd rather she stay safe."

Clint, looking out the window at the quickly darkening sky, couldn't help feeling Josie was in more danger now than ever. Hell, he was so worried he could swear he even heard her calling for help. Calling for . . .

"Fuck! Call the ranch."

"Why?" asked Brandon, and then his eyes widened. "You heard it, too. I thought I was imagining her call for help." He whipped out his cell phone and rang the house, but after six rings, voicemail picked up. He dialed the numbers of the wolves left to guard, but they all went to a busy signal.

Clint didn't need to talk to someone to know Josie was in danger. He sped the SUV through traffic, weaving in and out, racing as quickly as he dared and then some.

He knew they were too late as soon as he pulled up to the ranch and saw the note pinned to the door. He ran for the porch, his booted feet thumping as he pounded up the steps. He tore the note from the door, chills shaking him to the core as he saw the familiar handwriting.

He ignored Brandon, who leaned over his

shoulder reading along with him, fear and anger battling for supremacy.

I've taken the bitch, and the choice is simple. Present yourselves to me and swear yourself into my service, and she goes free. Fight or avoid my summons, and she dies. Simple enough even you mongrels should grasp it. Come and pay fealty to your new master at the refinery. The choice whether she lives or dies is yours. And, might I add, if you choose her death, it will be a bloody and painful one.

Clint couldn't stop it. He howled, a rage-filled sound whose deadly challenge rose to hang in the night sky and was echoed by his beta.

"It dies," Clint growled, his humanity losing the battle against the fierce anger of his beast. His fingernails elongated into claws, and rippling muscle and flesh tore through the fabric he wore.

But Clint fought the urges of his wolf—the need to protect his mate. If they were to survive, he needed to think. He didn't for one moment believe that the bastard toying with them would let Josie go.

Brandon, who'd lost the battle with his wolf, whined beside him.

Clint looked down at his furry blond friend. "I need to call in the pack before we go. We need them to take out the guards while we take care of the one in charge." In other words, tear the fucker limb from limb.

It didn't take long for him to send out a blanket text message to the pack. He didn't wait for their answer. They would show up as instructed or face his wrath after.

Clint looked down at his ragged garments and vetoed changing. No point in possibly ruining two sets of clothes. Besides, he kept spare outfits for emergencies stashed in his SUV.

Clint opened the back tailgate so Brandon could jump in. Clint slid back into the driver seat and stomped the gas. Gravel went flying as the SUV fishtailed around and flew back up the drive.

Too angry to think—and scared for Josie—he tried to concentrate on sensing her again. But he heard nothing else, and that frightened him even more than the note. *What if she's already dead? No, she can't be. I'd know if she was. But, fuck, she's got to be terrified, especially if, as I suspect, the bogeyman behind her nightmares has her. Please don't let me be too late.*

The miles sped by in the darkness as Clint maneuvered the SUV through the back roads leading to the abandoned refinery. A place that a pair of his men had checked and concluded abandoned for a while. The same pair of men who'd taken over the last protective guard detail and who were now missing.

Dammit, they probably stumbled onto the bastard, and he messed with their minds just like he did with those rogues. He was pissed at himself for not realizing the possibility sooner. He'd pushed aside the weird mind-control issue, assuming the rogues had been weak and easily taken over. He'd underestimated the enemy, and Josie now paid the price for his mistake.

Hold on, baby. I will make this right. I swear.

He drew into the vacant parking lot of the abandoned refinery. He didn't bother hiding his arrival. If the message had gotten out, then his wolves would be arriving by stealth to surround the place. Or so he hoped. His drive from the ranch should have taken longer than it took his troops to get there on furry feet, but he dared not search for or contact them. Nor did he have the patience to wait, not while Josie remained in peril.

He opened the rear hatch, and Brandon, the fur of his beast bristling, jumped out. Before he could tell Brandon to wait, he took off.

Clint followed more cautiously. He wouldn't do anyone any good dead. He debated changing shapes but decided against it for the moment. Even when he wore his human form, his senses were heightened.

The derelict building loomed over him, and he had no difficulty finding a door to enter. Once inside, he inhaled deeply and almost gagged. The alien stench he'd smelled before when Josie dreamed permeated the air, a sickening smell. Melted into it he found tendrils of wolf, some familiar to him, along with other scents that reminded him of other shifters he'd encountered over the years. He also caught the scent of Josie.

He separated her smell from the others and followed it, its faint trail leading him to a dark doorway with stairs leading down. He moved down the steps, the oppressive stench of the one who wanted to be master pressing down on him, trying to twist his thoughts. However, Clint hadn't become alpha because he was weak. Actually, the attempt to fuck with his mind made him seethe with anger, which strengthened him. He easily repelled the suggestion to surrender that hovered in the air. *You're going to have to do better than that, you bastard.*

He'd almost reached the bottom when he

heard Josie whimper, the sound faint, yet his wolf recognized it, and the terror that underlay it.

With a roar, his beast took over. Instinct drove him to run toward his mate, the protective need too strong to control. It barreled him right into a trap.

Snarling bodies slammed into him, but Clint wouldn't allow them to keep him from his woman. *She needs me, and they're in my way.*

With a roar, he tore into the snapping mob, only vaguely noticing Brandon's arrival. Together they battled, the sharp tear of their teeth and stronger bodies overcoming the paltry force sent to stop them.

When the last body dropped, with wheezes and whines, Clint raced down the hall, sensing Josie's nearness. Brandon followed at his heels. Just before a gaping archway, Clint halted. The alien miasma peppered with Josie's sweeter essence poured forth, and Clint knew he'd found them. Clint shifted back to his man shape, his expression grim.

I'm here, baby. Just hold on, and I'll make sure the nightmare is over, permanently.

Chapter Twenty

Josie woke in a basement—a cold, dank, and in need of a major renovation basement. Of course, part of the reason for her chill could have had to do with the fact that she found herself surrounded by dangling cocoons, big human-shaped ones. Not exactly a reassuring sign.

Great, my nightmare has evolved. Even as she tried to fool herself into thinking she slept, she knew better. From the frigid air that made her breath puff out in white clouds to the pain in her body from the attack and kidnapping, the sensations were impossible to ignore. *I'm awake, and that doesn't bode well.*

Clint and Brandon were probably frantic and furious, but how could they have known that one of their own pack would be susceptible? *I am so stupid. I knew Snickers wouldn't go outside. She hates grass.* Blaming herself accomplished nothing, except keep at bay, for a tiny moment more, the throat-closing fear that froze her limbs, not that they could move in the first place, bound tight in the sticky threads of a cocoon, it was her nightmare made real.

A match flared and lit the tip of a taper. Josie blinked at the sudden illumination then wished she'd closed her eyes tight and never opened them. In the circular glow cast by the candle stood a hooded figure, and even though she'd only just recently begun to believe in things science could not explain, there was no denying that the cold waves rolling off the figure were evil.

Welcome to my nightmare. She should have told him there was no need to bind her. Why, when terror had her paralyzed? The cowled one strode forward. The malice flowing from its body intensified, and Josie shook.

She wanted to scream when a pale hand rose and a finger with a sharp fingernail dragged across her skin. She bit her lip at the pain when he pressed down harder, breaking her skin.

"So glad you could make it." The voice, sibilant and low, rocked her with its familiarity; it was a voice from her nightmares, usually forgotten upon waking.

"Why me?" she whispered as tears rolled down her cheeks.

"You're mine, and I've been looking for you for a long time," was the chilling reply.

"I don't understand. What's so special about me?" Josie asked, her words coming out in a wail.

The bogeyman inhaled deeply. "I love the smell of fear. And yours is especially delicious. As to your question of why, I need your wolves, among other things."

Josie's breath left her. *Clint and Brandon?* "No. I won't let them. I'd rather die," she said in a moment of bravery, unable to bear even thinking of them coming to harm, especially not because of her. *I'm not worth them sacrificing themselves to this…this thing.*

"Die? Who said anything about dying? You, my dear, have something I want. Something your bitch of a mother denied me."

Confusion creased her brow, and for a moment, fear eased its hold to curiosity. "What does my mother have to do with anything? She's dead."

"The bitch would deny me by dying before I could find her. You see your mother was my fiancée a long time ago, not by choice. Her father arranged the match for a price of course. And I paid his hefty fee, for, you see, your mother was the carrier of a very rare condition, a state that made her destined to be mine. I would have made her my queen. Instead, the slut ran off with a human of all things. By the time I found where she'd fled and hidden, she'd died. Lucky me, though, she left behind a daughter, one with the same dormant power. "

Images of her mother, few as she had, flashed through her mind, filled with smiles and laughter, but even though she'd been a child, Josie remembered her fear when someone knocked at the door. *Could he be telling the truth?* "I don't understand. My mother was human. You have the wrong person."

"Your mother was a liar," he shouted. Cadaverous hands pushed back his hood to reveal a face that should have remained in shadow. Gray skin stretched across sharp cheeks, and bloodless lips peeled back from teeth sharpened to points. Josie couldn't help shuddering when he grinned at her, the rictus of amusement stretching his face grotesquely and lighting the fires of madness in his eyes.

Josie forced herself to speak, even as she beheld the face of evil. "I don't believe you. I would have known if she was special. She would have told me." *I know she would have, had she lived and not died unexpectedly in that car crash.*

A cold smile met her refutation. "Poor, deluded child. You know I speak the truth. I can see the dawning of understanding in your eyes. Your mother was the rarest of rare. A true shapeshifter, able to become anything she wanted."

Josie closed her eyes against the knowledge. *My mother was a shapeshifter. No wonder Clint and Brandon were attracted to me. It's in my genes. Not that they'll ever know now.* Much as a part of her hoped for rescue, she prayed they'd be smart and stay away.

"While I've enjoyed our little chat, it's time for silence. Your suitors have arrived to try and save you. Predictable dogs. Never fear. Once I've taken care of them, I will make you the recipient of my full attention. After I cleanse your body of their touch, that is. I need a clean receptacle for my seed."

Josie could only whimper pathetically as the monster disguised as a man shrugged off his robe, which revealed a pale, emaciated body. His body rippled as he shifted into the eight-legged monster that had terrorized her dreams for so long.

Josie hiccupped in fear, a sound silenced as he spun a web across her mouth but leaving her nose and eyes uncovered. She watched with running tears as Clint and Brandon sauntered in, big, bold, and beautiful. They'd come for her. *Oh, how I wish they hadn't and saved themselves instead.* She'd known, though, deep down, they would never allow her kidnapping to go unanswered.

She saw their bodies—naked as if they'd just

shifted back—stiffen in outrage when they perceived her. She tried to tell them with her eyes to run, escape while they could. They didn't all need to die today.

The stubborn jerks, so brave and wonderful, would never turn tail and run.

Oh, how I wish I could have one last chance with them, to tell them how much I love them both.

Chapter Twenty-one

Brandon growled when he saw Josie, terrified and crying. His anger exploded at finding her trussed and strung up like an appetizer for later. He couldn't stop his beast from bursting forth. His hackles rose in stiff spikes along his spine as he watched the arachnid shifter who'd caused so much havoc and terrorized his woman. *I'm going to tear your legs off one by one, you fucking bastard.*

Beside him, Clint's body went rigid, and his voice when he addressed the cadaverous man in front of them was the low, controlled tone of a man in the grips of white rage. "Release our woman."

The immense spider shifted back into its human form—not a prettier sight. With a cold smile, the shifter opened his arms wide. "What kind of greeting is that? In case you hadn't noticed, you're in my home. I realize your pea-sized canine brains might not be able to grasp it, but I am the one in control here. I will decide what happens."

"This is your last chance. Let her go if you want to live." Clint spat the words out through stiff lips, his fists clenched at his side. Brandon marveled at his control.

The spider shifter laughed, a rusty sound that held no mirth. "What, aren't you going to chivalrously offer to trade yourselves for her? And you call yourself her lovers."

Clint took a step forward and cocked his head. "Drop the pretense. We both know you never intended to let her go. All the scare tactics, those weren't meant for us. She was the one you wanted all along."

"Give a prize to the talking doggie," said the voice of evil as he clapped. His eyes blazed as he hissed at them. "Stupid mutts. You had the biggest reward of all, and you never even realized it."

"That's because, in our eyes, Josie isn't a prize but a person, one whom we cherish."

The nasty being chuckled. "Weaklings. And to think you're what stands between me and ownership of this city. Not for long. Once I kill you, control of the pack will fall to me."

"And just how do you plan to kill me?" Most people, when confronted in the buff, would appear in a position of weakness, but naked and cocky, Clint looked dangerous. And if Brandon's wolf could have grinned, it would have.

Here we go. It's about to start.

Brandon knew Clint taunted the arachnid on purpose. They'd discussed their plan before going in. In a nutshell, Clint would distract the bad guy while Brandon freed Josie. A great plan, if it worked. But unlike the trap on the way against shifters whose minds were controlled by the spider, fighting this creature would be more treacherous. For one, they'd have to be on constant guard—in their minds. Since they'd entered its lair, Brandon had felt the pressure pounding against his thoughts, insidious whispering that oozed along the walls in his psyche looking for a breach point.

In the midst of battle, how much harder would it be to prevent the slippery, evil tendrils from entering?

Not that it mattered. They'd both do anything to free the little mouse who'd taken over their hearts. Death paled in comparison to a life without her.

And the deciding moment had arrived. Clint said something that finally pushed the alien shifter over the edge. With a high-pitched cry, the cadaverous body was replaced with his alter ego, the eight-legged freak.

Clint had also allowed his wolf to burst free, and as he ran, snarling at the arachnid, Brandon quickly made his way toward Josie.

Brandon forced himself to look away from her face as he used his teeth to tear through the silken threads binding her. He didn't want to be distracted. Sticky and stronger than it appeared, the cocoon didn't shred as rapidly as he would have liked. Behind him, he could hear the sounds of battle as Clint fought the beast alone.

Once Josie's arms and legs were freed, Brandon shifted long enough to say "Go! Run! Get in the SUV, and get away from here." Brandon pushed her in the direction of the stairs.

She hesitated. "But what about you and Clint?"

"Piece of cake." Brandon gave her a cocky grin and a hard kiss before shoving her again toward the stairs. A yelp made them both turn. Clint limped back from the monstrous spider, blood streaming from a wide gash in his side. *Time to squish the spider.*

Chapter Twenty-two

"Run," Brandon ordered her before he ran toward the nightmare battle, his pale buttocks flashing until he shifted back into his wolf shape.

Josie stayed rooted to the floor. She couldn't stop herself from watching. As wolves, Brandon and Clint were magnificent. Even injured, Clint lunged at the massive spider from one side while Brandon worried at it from the other. But the freak of nature was wily, not to mention multi-limbed. It batted them away to bloody effect. Its many faceted eyes glowed red, and from its maw dripped a slime that made Brandon yelp when it touched his skin.

They needed help. But the only person left was her. *I can't do this. I can't. Oh my God.*

Even as she whimpered in terror, she picked up a rusted piece of metal, its end jagged and dangerous. She forced herself on legs that shook to approach the spider. It turned its nightmarish head toward her, and even in its inhuman guise, she heard it chuckle. Whispers swirled around her, sibilant sounds that taunted her and made her whole body tremble. So focused was she on ignoring the voices she didn't see the hairy leg that arched out. She couldn't miss feeling it, though.

Its clawed tip jabbed her in the stomach and

knocked her down. As she lay there, stunned, pain spread its eager claws throughout her body. She heard howling, an eerie sound that preceded the invigorated sounds of battle.

Josie tried to push herself up, but the agony proved too much, and she slumped back.

Is this how I die?

Her fingers scrabbled against the hard floor and encountered the metal lance she'd dropped. She grasped it, only one thought in her mind—save the ones she loved.

She waited for her moment, free of fear for once in her life. Calm as a windless day, she prepared to face the end.

But not alone. When the lumbering body of the spider straddled her as it backed away from an intense attack, she gathered her last reserves of strength—and the love she carried for Clint and Brandon—and shoved the spear up through the soft underbelly of the beast.

The gushing ichor burned as it splashed down on her. Not that she noticed. Out of strength, she closed her eyes.

Chapter Twenty-three

Unbelievable. Clint couldn't believe his eyes when he saw Josie—sweet, timid Josie—brave her fear and come back to help them. He didn't have time to shift and yell at her to run away, but he saw with horrible clarity the leg that shot out to stab her in the stomach. She dropped to the floor, and a red film descended over his eyes. Grief and anguish gave him new energy, and he attacked the spider that wouldn't die. He and Brandon had scored numerous hits on the beast, and while it leaked bodily fluids, they had yet to weaken it.

It didn't help that his mind was in a constant battle to remain unfettered. The arachnid's powers of persuasion were unbelievable, and Clint was thankful that the rest of the pack was busy elsewhere engaging the rogues and thus preventing the spider from calling its reinforcements.

A vicious swipe, which he failed to dodge, staggered him. Shaking his head though, Clint and his wolf refused to give up. He prepared to run the leg gauntlet again, seeking the soft underbelly and the heart of the creature. The spider skittered back, right over Josie's still body. Clint howled in renewed anguish.

Then the miracle happened.

Incredulous, he could only watch as Josie, not dead after all, stirred beneath the arachnid. With her face contorted and her eyes squeezed shut in fear, she screamed as she thrust up with a jagged rod of metal. At the sound of a high-pitched squeal, Clint knew she'd hit the mark. As the light in the spider's eyes faded, Clint, with a burst of speed, leaped at the bulky body that slowly folded downward. His momentum was enough to send the teetering corpse sideways and away from Josie, even as she exclaimed "gross" in response to the gushing fluids.

He had no sooner hit the floor than he shifted to a human and ran to Josie, who'd barely missed getting squished. Her courageous act must have sucked at the last of her reserves, for she now lay still as death. As he scanned her body, Clint howled, for her injuries were numerous.

Brandon, who'd also shifted back, knelt beside him, his face twisted in grief. "Dammit, Clint, do something. She's dying."

I know she is, but how do I stop death? Clint gathered up her bleeding body, and tears pricked his eyes—unmanly perhaps, but he couldn't help them. *And Josie thought she wasn't brave.* He'd never seen anything more courageous in his life than her confronting her all-too-real nightmare. In that moment, he knew what to do. He just didn't know if she'd survive it. However, if he didn't try, she'd die for sure. "We need to shift and bite her."

Brandon looked over at him with red-rimmed eyes. "But that could kill her."

"She's dead if we don't," Clint replied grimly.

Brandon stared down at her then glanced

back to face Clint. "Both of us?"

"We haven't marked her as our mate yet. Are you prepared to lose her as a mate if my bite alone alters the bond? Besides, it's bound to be more potent if she receives the bite from two of us." Or twice as deadly.

"Enough said."

Clint lay her back down and shifted, as did Brandon. They both grasped her lower forearm in their jaws, and he projected one thought to Brandon before he bit down. *"Now!"*

As soon as Clint tasted the metallic tang of her blood, he backed off and shifted back. He and Brandon sat on their haunches, naked, bruised, and dirty, and waited to see if their action would save or kill the one they loved.

For a moment, Clint thought they'd failed. Her breathing slowed, her skin turned waxy.

Then she scared the crap out of him.

She let out a strident scream and arched her back. Clint and Brandon dove for her, trying to hold her down, but her body, in the grips of the change, one like he'd never heard of, bucked them off. They could only watch as she thrashed on the ground. And then the most disturbing—perhaps even amazing—thing happened.

She shifted into a wolf, then a bear, then a bird, then a panther. Almost too quick to see, her body morphed into a dizzying amount of shapes, and Clint finally understood what the spider had meant when he'd said Josie was a prize.

Clint had heard of them—shapeshifters who could adopt any shape—but like many, he'd thought them legend.

Dozens, then hundreds, of shifts later, Josie resumed her human body, naked and without a single damn blemish to mark her ordeal.

There was only one problem. She wouldn't wake up.

Chapter Twenty-four

Nothing better than being woken with kisses. Josie smiled as her lovers slid their bodies across hers, the skin-to-skin contact ensuring she tingled from head to toe.

Then she remembered what had happened. Her eyes shot open as she sat up abruptly. She looked down to her stomach and gaped at her unblemished skin.

"You're healed," stated Clint.

"But how?" she asked as she turned her attention to her men as they lay on their backs in her bed back at the ranch. They grinned as she ran her hands over their bodies, searching for injuries that didn't exist, well, except for a few red scar lines.

"We're shifters. We healed," said Brandon, who shrugged.

"I'm not, though," she said, puzzled, for she still clearly remembered the burning pain of her injury.

"Yeah, well, about that. We had to bite you to save you."

Josie gaped at them. "You did what?"

"It was the only way. You were dying. We couldn't let that happen."

"So, I'm a werewolf like you now?" she said,

remembering what they'd told her.

"Not exactly," Clint hedged.

Josie narrowed her eyes. "Explain."

Brandon spoke first. "Um, how well do you know your parents?"

The words of the spider shifter came back to her, and her eyes widened. "My mother. He said she could shift into anything she wanted. But I guess up until now, the power was dormant in me."

"Not anymore," announced Clint.

"You mean I can be any animal I want?"

"Yes, but you'll probably have to practice. Don't worry. We'll help you learn."

I'm a shapeshifter! Josie waited for her usual anxiety to grip her. Momentous news usually did it to her. But to her surprise, nothing happened. The enormous ball of tension she'd lived with so long was gone. She felt free, and beaming at her two very naked lovers, she found herself in the grips of another emotion. Make that urge.

"Sounds good, but can we do it later? I've got something else I need to practice first."

"What's that?" asked Brandon, the carnal interest in his eyes matched by his rising cock.

Clint moved behind her and pushed aside her hair to kiss her nape. "I think Josie's ready to try what we talked about."

"Among other things." Josie crooked her finger at Brandon, who went to his knees in front of her. His hard cock poked her in the belly, and a gushing warmth moistened her cleft.

She found his mouth with hers, initiating a kiss that had him panting in moments, probably because she'd also grabbed the throbbing shaft that jabbed her and stroked it. She broke the kiss and leaned her head back to offer her mouth to Clint. He kissed her hard as he slid his hands around her waist and up to cup her breasts.

Josie moaned when Brandon found her clit with his index finger and rubbed it. She lost control of the situation but didn't care as they pushed her down onto the bed. She opened her eyes when she felt her arms pulled above her head and held in a strong grip. She gazed up at Clint, who smiled wickedly at her. She returned his smile. Brandon, kneeling between her thighs, pushed her legs up and apart, exposing her. She couldn't help the blush that stained her cheeks, and Clint chuckled.

"Oh, baby, you are so damned cute."

She would have replied, but Brandon chose that moment to run his wet tongue up her silken slit. Her back arched, but the rest of her stayed locked, held down by her men who seemed determined to make this a moment to remember.

Brandon buried his face against her sex and lapped from her like a man parched. Josie panted and mewled, the exquisite strokes of his tongue driving her quickly mounting pleasure too high, too fast. She fought to hold on, to prolong the pleasure, but when Clint shifted his position and latched his mouth onto a tight nipple, the extra sensation was too much.

Her climax exploded, and she screamed.

Slowly, the waves calmed, but her body felt like a wire wound too tight. One erotic move and it would shatter again.

"That's my girl," murmured Clint before

biting down on her nipple, sending a pleasurable jolt down to her cunt.

Brandon, between her thighs, his tongue still busy, groaned in agreement.

"Too much," she finally managed to gasp. With a chuckle, Clint released her nipple and captured her lips instead.

Brandon's mouth stopped its torture as well, but only so he could change tactics. Something slapped against her clit, and Josie jumped, almost biting Clint.

Again and again, Brandon slapped and rubbed the head of his swollen cock across her clit. The fire they'd just sated built up again, and suddenly she found herself astride Clint, his rigid rod poking at her sex.

"Ride me, baby." His smoky eyes held hers as he lifted her and seated her on his cock. Her channel, so wet, took his thick length easily and, perched atop him, so deep.

Josie gasped and dug her fingers into Clint's chest. From behind, Brandon cozied up to her back, the head of his prick poking at her back door. Clint distracted her by gripping her hips and sliding her forward then back hard.

The motion bumped the head of his cock, buried deep, against her sweet spot. Back and forth he slid her, almost managing to distract her from the wet finger that probed at her rosette.

It felt strange, not bad exactly but different. She felt a cold dribble down the crack of her cheeks and wondered at it until the added lube allowed Brandon to pop his finger in.

"Oh." She couldn't prevent the gasp as her tight ring stretched to accommodate the intruding finger. Uncomfortable, she squirmed.

"Push out against it," growled Brandon. She did and found the pressure eased somewhat. Before she could decide if she liked it or not, he popped a second in. She went still, really not sure anymore about this intrusion.

"Bend over and kiss him," Brandon ordered, his voice strained.

Josie obeyed, leaning forward until her breasts brushed Clint's chest. His head rose to meet hers, and their lips joined in a scorching kiss. Bent forward like this exposed her back door, and Brandon used this to his advantage, working a third finger in, making it even tighter. Her body had made the transition since the first probing digit from uncomfortable to exciting, erotically so. With Clint's cock still sheathed in her sex, Josie found herself rocking back against the fingers in her second hole and enjoying it.

As if this were a signal, the fingers slipped out, only to be replaced by something thicker. She lost herself in Clint's kiss, trying to ignore the pushing pressure at her rosette. She did cry out when Brandon finally popped the head of his rod past the tight ring. Big and too tight, that was the only thing she could think of. Worry was forgotten as Clint thrust his hips up into her while Brandon reached under to twist and tweak her nipples.

Overwhelmed with pleasure, she relaxed, and Brandon eased his cock in to the hilt. Josie's sex spasmed at the full sensation, quivers that repeated as the guys set a rhythm where one withdrew while the other plowed in. Josie, caught between their bodies, just enjoyed the ride.

How could she not? The rub of their skin against hers. The feel of Clint's and Brandon's mouths on her neck. The pleasing fullness of their thrusting cocks. The sensory overload of her G-spot being struck. Her body tightened, squeezing them, and as she hit the peak, they bit down on her neck while their cocks spurted hotly within her.

Pain. Pleasure. Heat. And incredible bliss. Josie didn't have enough breath left to scream as the orgasm of all orgasms rolled over her. And over again. And . . .

It took her a while to come back down from such bliss, and when she did, she found herself sandwiched between them.

"Wow." *What else is there to say?*

Clint chuckled. "No kidding."

"So, when are we going for a repeat?" joked Brandon.

Josie moaned. "Oh my God, I don't think I'll ever move again." At his chagrined look, she smiled mischievously. "But don't worry. As soon as I convince my body to work again, I'm all for trying again."

Laughter sounded as they all gave in to mirth. After all, what wasn't there to be happy about? One nagging thing. And Josie, the new and improved Josie, found the courage to broach it first.

"I know we're mated now and everything, but I wanted to say, mate or not, I . . ." She swallowed, and tears pricked her eyes as she bravely said the words in her heart. "I love you, Clint. And I love you, Brandon, and I am so glad you've chosen me as your mate, even if I'm not a wolf or a bombshell or . . ."

Clint placed a callused finger on her lips and stopped her. "Oh, baby, haven't you figured it out yet? We love you, every adorable, sexy part of you."

"What's not to love?" said Brandon, his tousled blond hair contrasting against Clint's dark crown as they both stared down at her. In their eyes, she saw the love she craved. And the smoldering heat that promised untold future pleasure.

"Well, in that case, how about we have a shower, and after we've locked the doors against visitors, you show me in front of a roaring fire just how much?"

Of course the shower led to slippery, soapy fun. And the impromptu dinner tested the sturdiness of the breakfast bar. But when they did eventually make it to the rug in front of the roaring flames, they showed her and told her just how much she was loved.

Epilogue

Impatience gripped Josie. She couldn't wait to show them. How pleased they would be, if miffed at what she'd hidden. But she wanted it to be a surprise, which was why she practiced in secret with the help of a female pack member who'd befriended her over the last few weeks. It still blew her away to know that she was special now, and not just because she could change into any animal or beast she wanted, although that helped.

Every day with words, actions, and thoughtful gestures designed to make her smile, her men showed her just how appreciated she truly was. And like a flower parched for want of moisture, she soaked it up and bloomed.

My turn to give something back. When she trotted out to see them where they waited for her on the front porch, the look on their faces was worth the struggle to learn how to use the powers she'd acquired.

"Oh, baby, you're gorgeous," whispered Clint.

Brandon's eyes shone with appreciation, and he let out a piercing whistle.

With no care for their clothes, they shifted into their wolves and approached her for a nuzzle. Grinning with her new canines, she yipped at them and took off running, her joyous howl echoed by her lovers who chased after.

How wonderful and amazing my life is now. Her previous fears over just about anything had yet to come back to plague her. It was a wonder what battling a giant spider could do for a girl's courage. *Actually, as it turned out, I always had courage; I just needed the incentive of love to bring it out. And guess what? I'm no longer scared of spiders.*

The End

Author Bio

Hello and thank you so much for reading my story. I

hope I kept you well entertained. As you might have noticed, I enjoy blending humor in to my romance. If you like my style then I have many other wicked stories that might intrigue you. Skip ahead for a sneak peek, or pay me a visit at http://www.EveLanglais.com This Canadian author and mom of three would love to hear from you so be sure to connect with me.

Facebook: http://bit.ly/faceevel
Twitter: @evelanglais
Goodreads: http://bit.ly/evelgood
Amazon: http://bit.ly/evelamz
Newsletter: http://evelanglais.com/newrelease

Printed in Great Britain
by Amazon